Scarlet Birthright

WHAT THEY LEFT BEHIND

Scarlet Ibis James

DKJ Enterprises LLC

DISCOVERY AND KEY, NEW YORK
A SUBSIDIARY OF DKJ ENTERPRISES

Scarlet Birthright, Stories of Love and Desire.

eBook ISBN: 979-8-9915909-5-2
Paperback ISBN: 979-8-9915909-7-6
Hardcover ISBN: 979-8-9915909-8-3
Audiobook ISBN: 979-8-9915909-9-0

Scarlet Birthright: What They Left Behind

Praise For Scarlet Birthright:
What They Left Behind

Scarlet Birthright is a raw, emotional novella about love, abandonment, regret, and redemption.

Winner, Literary Titan Gold Book Award
Winner, Independent Author Network Book of the Year Award
Winner, NYC Big Book Award
Winner, Readers' Favorite International Book Award
Finalist, Reedsy Discovery Book Awards

"Perhaps the book's greatest strength lies in James's imaginative use of shifting perspectives to create a panoply of voices that reveal the full emotional cost of Joromi's decision." — **BookShelfie**, *starred editorial review*

"A raw, emotional novella about love, abandonment, regret, and redemption … messy, real, and haunting in the best way." — **Literary Titan**, *starred editorial review*

"A riveting tale about love, family, and figuring out where you belong … I devoured this book in one sitting." — **Readers' Favorite**, *starred editorial review*

"A rich, multigenerational Caribbean saga that punches you in the chest then hugs you afterward — this is a must-read." — **The Bourbon-Sipping Bibliophile**

"A captivating and heartfelt story that spans generations and continents... rich with Caribbean storytelling traditions and offers a perfect blend of love, regret, and self-discovery." — **Amazon Reviewer**

Scarlet Birthright: What They Left Behind

To the spirits who keep vigil over my shoulders,

To the stories that refuse to sleep,

And to the children who inherit their parents' silences and songs.

"There is a crack somewhere in our spirits, and we have to heal that before anything."

—ANTONIO MICHAEL DOWNING, *Saga Boy: My Life of Blackness and Becoming*

Contents

Foreword

Stories, like children, sometimes choose their own paths.

When I initially wrote "The First Time I Met My Father" for my collection *Scarlet Yearnings: Stories of Love and Desire* (2024), I thought I had captured a complete moment — a young girl's first encounter with the father who had chosen absence over presence.

The response from readers was immediate and overwhelming. They wanted — needed — to know more. *Why the absence? What happened to the little girl?* But it wasn't just the readers who demanded these answers. The characters themselves began to speak to me, their voices as insistent as the Kiskadee bird's call, as persistent as the chords of a steelpan in the distance on a breeze.

They whispered their truths into my heart, becoming fleshy prose of autobiographical fiction. Like the Caribbean Sea, the stories held depths that demanded exploration.

Like the islands of Trinidad and Tobago, these

characters move through distinct seasons that shape their experiences. Our islands know two rhythms: the dry season from January to May, when the heat sits heavy and still, baking the earth and invigorating our souls, and the rainy season from June to December, when the air grows thick with humidity, testing our resolve. The dry season's heat is sharp and clarifying, forcing us to face formidable truths under an unrelenting sun. The rainy season's heat is different—it wraps around you like a second skin, making everything feel more urgent, demanding shifts.

Each chapter in this story is marked by these seasons, not just as measures of time but as mirrors of the characters' inner weather.

Joromi's story begins in the dry season of 1969, when certainty burns away like the morning mist, leaving him to face choices as ominous as shadows at noon. Young and fierce, he needed to explain why love sometimes frightens more than failure. The rainy season brings Trisha's early memories, humid with longing and rich with growth, carrying her own story and the legacy of a mother she never knew and a father she was only beginning to understand. Even the grandparents—steady Cecil and wise Mary—had the wisdom to tell me how love transforms when we learn to let it breathe, their story flowing through both seasons like the island's lifeblood.

This novella also travels across seas and space to land in the United States of America. For Joromi and Margaret in New York, winter and spring brought rhythms utterly foreign to their Trinidad-born souls. The harsh winter months tested their marriage as they huddled in their small apartment, the cold seeping through windows and forcing them closer together — physically, if not emotionally. For Joromi, each snowfall seemed to blanket his memories of Trinidad, while Margaret found strength in the stark clarity of snow-laden streets, using the season's stillness to build their American dream piece by piece.

When spring finally arrived, it stirred something in Joromi that felt dangerously like home — the way new buds emerged in Central Park reminded him of Trinidad's dry season when even the most reluctant plants found ways to bloom. Margaret watched him during these moments, seeing how the warming air made him more restless, more prone to playing his old calypso records when he thought she wasn't listening. Together, they navigated these new seasons, each finding their way to transplant their Caribbean roots into foreign soil.

Scarlet Birthright is more than just an answer to a question posed in my previous work. It is a testament to how stories, like the Cascadura fish of Trinidad legend, can call us back to places we thought we'd left behind. It explores how passion, fear, and courage flow through generations like blood and how sometimes the greatest act of love is learning to choose differently than those who came before us.

To my readers who asked for this story — thank you for your curiosity and faith. To these characters who refused to remain silent — thank you for trusting me with your truths. And to all those who open these pages, I invite you to discover how one summer's passion in Port of Spain in 1969 ripples through time to touch a daughter's heart in 1991 and, perhaps, your own heart, too.

At the end of this novella, you'll find both the

acknowledgments and the Soul Clef, a glossary of Trinidad and Tobago's rich dialect and cultural terms. While you might be tempted to jump there whenever you encounter unfamiliar words, I encourage you to let the context guide you first. Like all profound truths, meaning often reveals itself slowly, layer by layer. The glossary stands ready as your companion, not your crutch—to deepen your understanding when needed but never to interrupt the story's natural flow.

Part One

Wildfire Season

Chapter 1—Joromi

May 1969, Dry Season

I was spinning records at my usual Friday night fête, riding high on the success of my latest party series. *Joromi Enoch, yuh on fire man!* I thought, dancing and smiling at the scene before me. The living room of my family's French colonial-style house had been transformed into a makeshift dance club, with about fifty people packed between the pushed-back furniture. Sweat gleamed on dancing bodies as my latest mix of funk, soul and calypso filled the space. At nineteen, I'd made a name for myself as the DJ who could read a crowd and who knew exactly when to drop the beat. Girls would come to watch me work the decks, and I won't lie — I enjoyed the attention. But tonight would be different.

Tonight would change everything.

The front door swung open, letting in a blast of warm night air. It carried the sweet scent of frangipani from our front yard. Every conversation came to a jarring stop like a needle yanked off a spinning record. No armor could defend me from what happened next.

Her.

She sashayed into the fête, swinging those hips seductively, then pausing in the doorway where the yellow porch light caught her silhouette. Her massive Afro, a halo of dark, untamed power, seemed to catch and trap the dim light of the room. The ceiling fan spun lazily overhead, stirring the air thick with music and cigarette smoke but she stood perfectly still, like she owned the moment.

My mind raced to categorize her and could not find any classification that would do her justice. Even the way she held her cowrie-beaded clutch — casual but commanding — made it clear she belonged anywhere she chose to be. A barely-there red minidress clung to her curves, skimming her shoulders, teasing the small swell of her breasts, and stopping just shy of scandal. It hugged her in a way that broke every rule — and made my nineteen-year-old self glad it did.

She stood in the doorway, scanning the crowded room like she was taking inventory. Her eyes moved methodically from the cluster of guys near the makeshift bar in the corner, past the couples swaying to the music in the center, to the girls perched on the arms of our old sofa. I recognized the look — she was checking the scene, deciding if this party was worth her time, as we all did back then. But there was something different about how she did it — no hesitation, no self-consciousness, only pure confidence.

Something intense ignited within me. It burned through the hidden guardrails of my mind. It hit like a rogue wave, leaving me stripped and exposed, raw in a way that was equal parts thrill and terror. My chest tightened, warmth spreading fast, and I felt like I'd been caught without armor — bare, vulnerable in the amber glow of the room.

I was confused because I was feeling things that were altogether new — besides the familiar rush of raw attraction I'd felt with other girls, there was something deeper. I wanted to explore every inch of her body, immerse myself in her thoughts, and be the only one to occupy her spirit.

What? What the hell is this?

As she completed her survey of the room, a hint of a smile touched her face. I was frozen, watching her.

The record on my turntable was ending, the bass line fading, but I couldn't move to change it.

Her eyes.

Eyes are paired sensory organs that detect light and enable vision. My brain, scrambling, latched onto Biology — my favorite subject. Reliable, logical, familiar. But at this moment, the clinical definition wasn't enough. Not even close.

Dark as night, smoldering with something molten beneath the surface. Her gaze seemed to glow through the haze of party lights and cigarette smoke. Lost in watching her, I'd forgotten about the record spinning on my turntable. The music cut off abruptly — the telltale scratch of silence made every head in a party turn toward the DJ.

"Eh eh! Like de man get stick!" Fitz shouted from near the bar, his laugh slashing through the silence. "De girl got you good, boy!"

Heat rushed to my face as titters bubbled through the crowd. My hands fumbled for the next record—James Brown's "Say It Loud"—and I dropped the needle with less than my usual flourish. The familiar groove filled the room, and people gradually turned back to their dancing, though I could still feel some amused glances thrown my way.

Only then did I dare to look up again.

She was moving through the crowd, navigating between dancing bodies with deliberate grace. Unlike the others who'd returned to their revelry, her eyes hadn't left me. Each step was measured, unhurried, like she had all night to close the distance between us.

I held my cup with dregs of Fernandes Black Label Rum tighter.

My throat went dry. My pulse flipped and twisted. But I couldn't look away—didn't want to look away—as she drew closer, each step making the rest of the party fade further into background noise.

That was it.

She assessed me. Measured me. Like I was one more thing in the room, something to conquer or dismiss.

Me? I wasn't used to being scrutinized, not like this. At six-foot-one, with shoulders broad from swimming and arms toned from hauling speakers and crates of records, I was usually checked out, not sized up. My close-cropped hair set off high cheekbones I'd inherited from my mother, and hours under the Trinidad sun had polished my skin to a rich copper tone. Girls said I was gorgeous. They'd whisper this to each other and then giggle like I wasn't supposed to hear.

Sure, they came to my parties for the vibe but also to watch me work the decks. Once, a girl told me I had a way of moving that made the music look visible — rolling my shoulders to the rhythm and letting the beat flow through my body as my hands worked the vinyl.

"The way yuh close yuh eyes and sway when yuh know a perfect mix was coming, yuh fingers would dance across the records, and then yuh does smile before dropping the beat we waiting for... *Lawd fadda!* Is like watching brown sugar melt into the rhythm."

Yes, I knew what I was working with and wasn't shy about it. Maybe that's why I carried myself the way I did. Shoulders back, chin up, like I was untouchable. *Overconfident? Maybe.* But it came easy when you had a mom like mine.

She treated me like her prince — too well, if you asked my father. "You can't raise a man like this and expect him to function in normal society," he'd grumble, pacing the kitchen in his work boots. He said it all the time, shaking his head like I'd already failed some invisible test of manhood.

My father was always on me about how I lived — too many girls, too little focus. "You can't juggle women like you juggling records," he'd say, his disappointment thick in every word. He wanted me to settle down, to find one woman I could build a future with.

"Pick sense from nonsense, boy," he'd bark. "You

need somebody who'll stand by you—not these girls you spinning 'round like they on a turntable."

To him, my life wasn't serious enough. And love? Love wasn't stormy or passionate—it was practical. Stable. Rooted in responsibility. "Stop playing games," he'd tell me. "Find a woman you can bring home. One who'll build with you, not just want to party through life."

And a conventional job was what he wanted for me most of all. Something with a steady paycheck and a title that would convey craft and success. Not a DJ, not a party-thrower. Not whatever this life I was carving out for myself was supposed to be.

But right then, standing there and gripping the record jacket like it was the only thing tethering me to the ground, I wasn't thinking about him or his lectures. I wasn't thinking about a so-called regular job or a set path.

I was thinking about this woman who strutted into my world. I felt like her long examination of me peeled away all the bravado I wore like a second skin.

Then she smiled.

She really smiled this time—not big, not flashy. The parting of her lush lips, revealing a peek of white teeth, sent electricity racing down my spine, settling low and dangerously in my body.

And then, before I could look away, she stepped onto the raised platform we'd built in the corner. The click of her heels brought her closer until she was near enough for me to catch the scent of the flowering clover perfume on her skin and see the subtle flutter of her pulse at her throat.

I was glad the turntables were between us because I realized two things then.

She was exactly my height in those heels, her eyes level with mine, making it impossible to escape her honey-dark gaze. And my body, when it came to her, had ideas of its own—wild, reckless ideas. I released the cup and the record jacket and grabbed the edge of the turntable stand until I could feel the metal edge pressing into my palms.

Lord help me, I thought, *This woman will be trouble.*

I had no idea just how right I was.

* * *

Our relationship blazed through the summer of '69. She was…*something else.* Having finished secondary school just a few weeks prior, she moved through life like every day was Carnival Monday—free and easy, no concerns about tomorrow. While her friends were all rushing to the University of the West Indies, teacher's training or nursing school, she'd laugh and say, "Why everybody in such a hurry to get old?"

I admit I was similar to her in this way. It had been two years since I graduated from high school, but a steady job had eluded me. My parties were my only source of income since my father cut me off to teach me a lesson in adulthood.

We spent afternoons hunting for new records in Port of Spain, her fingers trailing over album covers while she danced between the aisles, singing whatever caught her ear. The shop owner would watch her warily as she pulled record after record, but she'd flash that killer smile and say, "Nah man, life too sweet to be so serious!" Before long, he'd be letting her play whatever she wanted.

We'd escape to my parents' gallery in the evenings, listening to the transistor radio while my mother cooked inside. Sometimes, we walked 'round the Savannah as the sun set, our borrowed radio keeping us company. She'd talk about everything and nothing.

"Yuh doh fine de clouds looking like breadfruit?"…

"Ah feel ah go lime in England one day…"

or *"Maybe ah go work in meh uncle's rum shop."*

"But girl, what you planning to do?" I'd ask, my father's voice echoing in my head about the importance of direction, of purpose.

She'd throw back her head and laugh, her massive Afro catching the dying sunlight. "Doux-doux, my plan is to be happy," she'd say, twirling to the radio music. "Everything go sort itself out, *oui*. Why yuh so worried 'bout tomorrow when today sweet like sugarcane?"

Sometimes, the deep country dialect caught me off guard when she spoke—so different from my carefully cultivated "town" accent and the "proper" English my father insisted we use at home. Her "yuh" instead of "you," her "dat" instead of "that" revealed she wasn't from our middle-class world of French colonial houses and Catholic secondary school education. But there was something magnetic about how freely she spoke, how she let the honest sing-song lilt of Trinidad flow through her words without shame or pretense.

The first time we made love was under the stars in Carenage, on a massive blanket I'd borrowed from home. We were both virgins, fumbling and nervous but pressing on. The waves crashed against the shore, masking our whispered discoveries of each other. Afterward, she told me stories her grandmother used to tell her about the stars, mixing up the constellations but making up better stories until I was laughing too hard to correct her.

She started coming to all my Friday night fêtes after that. I'd catch glimpses of her while I worked the decks — dancing with abandon, pulling my prim friends into her orbit until even they forgot themselves.

"Come nah! Wine down low!" she'd call out, teaching them moves that would have their parents crossing themselves if they saw.

As usual, my father's words would reverberate in my head, *That one too young, too thoughtless. No kind of woman to build a life with.* But I'd watch her move, the way she made everyone around her come alive, and something in my chest would lighten.

After one particularly successful party, she didn't go home. We ended up in my bedroom, on that same blanket — freshly washed by my mother — on the floor because the bed would have made too much noise. Her kisses tasted like rum and freedom, and I found myself wanting to lose myself in both.

But it was the third time that changed everything.

We were at her place—a tiny one-room spot she used to escape her parents' rules about "proper young ladies." It sat at the edge of her brother's yard, right up against a sagging wooden fence. The walls were painted a fading turquoise, peeling in places, and the room smelled of the vanilla oil she loved, mixing with the lingering scent of the fried plantains she'd made us earlier.

A dusty, old single fan whirred lazily in the corner, fighting against the heat that pressed in through the open window. The calls of the island's frogs and distant calypso from a neighbor's radio drifted in with the night air. Her bed was small, pushed against the wall, covered in mismatched sheets that smelled of cocoa butter and her favorite jasmine perfume—a graduation gift she wore too liberally.

I had to close my eyes against the sensory overload. But I couldn't keep them closed—I needed to see her, to watch the way the single bulb cast shadows across her skin, making her look like something from a dream I wasn't sure I wanted to wake from.

The intensity between us was familiar now, but something was different. Her fingers traced my back like she was writing secrets on my skin, her lips brushing my neck with a tenderness that made my heart stutter. When she whispered, "Stay with me nah?" it wasn't with her usual playful tone—there was something deeper there that made me feel wanted by her in a way I hadn't been prepared for.

I turned over to stop her from marking my body any further. My arm floated away from her, and I nestled the back of my head in the palms of my hands.

Then, when she rolled over to lay half her body on

mine, the word "love" floated through my mind, and panic followed closely behind. My father's warnings screamed on loop: *Boy, you need a woman who knows where she is going in life. This one is still playing child games. It's time to stop making sport and get smart.*

I could not speak—dared not speak.

Instead, I stared at the cracked ceiling, listening to the fan's uneven rhythm, feeling her breath steady against my chest.

This isn't supposed to be real! She isn't supposed to matter this much.

When she finally fell asleep, I made my decision. I had to end it. She was too young and unformed—treating life like one long fête, with no thought for tomorrow. I should get someone more… settled. Someone with a plan. Someone my father would approve of.

So I started pulling away, spending less time with her, using my parents as an excuse for why she could not visit me, and finding reasons to avoid meeting up with her. Worse, when I was not spinning records at the parties I threw, I would dance with other girls or hang out outside with my boys.

She didn't take it quietly—nothing about her was ever quiet. I still remember her standing up to me in my parents' yard, voice rising as she demanded answers.

"WHY YUH DOING DIS? You ain't nothing but ah coward, yuh hear?!" she shouted, tears streaming down her face. "Yuh runnin' from me—we have somethin' dat actually matter—jus' because yuh father tell yuh so? Like yuh 'fraid to live!"

"Girl, I don't know what you talkin' about. We were just having fun. You read too much into it."

Whap!

The slap across my face stung but did not hurt as much as the truth in her words.

I watched her storm off and cut her from my life. Cold.

This is for the best. This is what a man should do.

Chapter 2—Joromi

July 1969, Rainy Season

The morning after she left, I found myself trapped at the kitchen table between my parents. The air was thick with disappointment and the smell of my mother's coffee. My father's work boots tapped an impatient rhythm against the floor tiles.

"Boy, how much money you make from that party last night?" My father's voice was sharp, slicing through the morning quiet.

I stared into my untouched tea. "Twenty-four dollars."

"Twenty-four dollars?" He barked out a laugh that held no humor. "Boy, that can't even buy groceries for the week! You really think that's a living? Playing records for pocket change while living under my roof, eating my food, and bringing *bacchanal* into my yard?"

"Cecil," my mother interjected softly, "the boy is trying—"

"Trying what?" He pushed back from the table, the legs of his chair scraping against the floor. "To be a professional party boy? To waste his life?" He turned to me, his face hard. "You think your mother and I worked our whole lives so you could play DJ and run around with these backward country girls?"

"The parties are temporary. I'm figuring things out—"

"Figuring things out?" He paced the kitchen, his anger filling the small space. "At your age, I was already working two jobs. Had my own place. Was planning my future."

My mother reached across the table, her hand warm on mine. "He's only nineteen, Cecil. Give him time."

"Time?" My father stopped pacing. "Well, time is something we don't have much of anymore."

He pulled an envelope from his back pocket, tossing it onto the table. "Got the job in St. Croix. We're moving next year."

The word "we" hung in the air like a question.

"All of us?" I asked, though something in his face already told me the answer.

"You're over eighteen," he said, his voice quieter now but no less cutting. "Can't get you on the family visa.

Besides," —he gestured toward the house—"looks like you've made your choice about your future."

My mother's hand squeezed mine, looking at me but speaking to my father. "Cecil, please—"

"No, Mary. Maybe this is what he needs. To stand on his own two feet. To learn what it means to be a man." He grabbed his lunch pail from the counter. "Can't play records forever, son. Life isn't a party."

The screen door slammed behind him, leaving me with my mother's worried eyes and a future instantly filled with holes.

"He wants what's best for you," she whispered, but her voice trembled. "He just... he dreams so big for you."

I nodded, unable to speak. Pulling away from her, I stood and went to my room. Leaning against the door, I closed my eyes to block out the morning sun glowing in. Outside, a rooster crowed—blissfully ignorant that my parents planned to leave me in this country. With that single revelation, the ground seemed to vanish beneath my feet, sending me freefalling into a future I could no longer see or trust.

Chapter 3—Joromi

August 1969, Rainy Season

I met the woman who would become my wife on a sunny day in Port of Spain. She was walking on Prince Street on her lunch break. As I exited Rhyners Record Shop and said something back to my friend behind me, I bounced into her.

No fireworks. Peace. *Humph. Joy?* We smiled, and a soft click went off in my head.

What is this?

She embodied what I knew my father wanted for me—an elegantly dressed young woman. Later, I learned that she also had clear plans and solid dreams. Although she was a couple of years older than me, I pursued her, taking care to keep her away from anything in my life that seemed juvenile. I wanted to rise to her expectations.

Late in the rainy season, her visions for our future unfolded like a map, each detail carefully marked. Her brother owned a trucking company in New York, and she'd already spoken to him about me.

"He needs someone he can trust to manage the day-to-day," she'd say, her voice warm with certainty. "You could still DJ at the Trini clubs on weekends."

She'd already started the paperwork for my immigration, knowing which forms to file and which offices to visit. She wanted to be a housewife, to create the kind of home she said a man like me deserved. Two children, she'd decided — a boy first, then a girl — a house in Brooklyn where other Trinidad families lived. *Everything is laid out, everything is planned.*

"It's time to tell my parents," I said one evening in the gallery of my childhood home, barefoot, shirt sticking to my back. The heat was oppressive and heavy like the night itself held a grudge against humanity on this island. Fans did their circular jobs inside, barely making a dent in the thick air. Outside, the streetlights cast weak rings of light that melted into the dark.

She sat across from me. Her soft, tiny feet were in my lap, and I rubbed them absently as she giggled happily, looking at me with pride and expectation. "If you feel it's time, sure. I trust you." Her voice was sweet and coaxing. She spoke like those well-educated Trinidadians who carefully measured their words in Queen's English. I wanted to lose myself in everything she said, but the night felt strange and charged. I soon realized that my spirit had sensed a foreboding minutes before it happened.

"Hello? Good night!"

A sharp, clear voice rang out, slicing through the heavy air like a cutlass.

Someone was at the gate.

Before I turned my head to see, I knew. It wasn't a guess—it was a certainty. She was back!

Lawd fadda!

The girl who'd danced into my fête that night four months ago, who'd made me forget my music, was standing at the entrance to my parents' home. And here I was with my girlfriend, the woman who promised me stability, security, and a future in which I could impress my father. A lady who stiffened beside me, her foot sliding from my lap, eyes narrowing like she already knew—felt—what was coming.

Her voice, barely audible yet piercing, asked me, "Who is she?"

Who is she?

Only then did I turn to confirm who I knew was at my family's compound.

What I saw shocked me, and I jumped to my feet without thinking. Just as quickly, a wave of emotions hit me, weighing me down. I felt shock, guilt, anger, and…everything. I collapsed into the veranda chair, my eyes fixed on the girl I had tried to forget. Yet, the decision she revealed to me this evening ensured I would never erase her.

Her midsection curved gently beneath her dress, just

enough to hint at the child growing within.

I sat paralyzed while my mind thrashed between two worlds: the future I'd planned, and this new, inescapable reality.

My mother heard the calls from the gate. Drama was the one thing she despised most, and the fact that it seemed to be unfolding in her yard, again, was enough to bring her storming out of the house, her sandals slapping against the floor with each step.

"Boy, what is this?" she demanded, her voice harsh.

I opened my mouth, but no words came.

Her gaze followed mine, squinting toward the entryway. When she saw the girl—saw what she carried— my mother's eyes widened, first in surprise, then understanding, disapproval and a thousand implicit chastisements, I was sure.

It didn't take her long to take control of the situation. My mother didn't wait for explanations; she didn't need them. She made two swift decisions.

"Margaret, it's time for you to go home," she said to my girlfriend, her tone leaving no room for argument. "Joromi's father will give you a ride since it's night, and this boy," her eyes snapped to me, "has some urgent business to take care of."

I still sat frozen, my mind spinning with ways to salvage my plans, my dreams of America, and my chance to become the man my father wanted me to be. Each heartbeat seemed to whisper, *Get away, make it to New York. You will fix everything from there.*

"Why are you standing there like you deaf, mute, and paralyzed?" My mother barked, the uncharacteristic tone of her voice punching through my haze as she issued her second order. "Go and bring that girl."

My mother retreated into the house, the screen door banging shut behind her, leaving me with the girl.

We sat alone under the ambient gallery light for the first time since I unceremoniously extricated her from my life. Muscle memory caused me to reach for her hand, but she jerked away, eyes blazing. She let out a loud, long suck of saliva through clenched teeth. *Steups.*

I adjusted myself in the chair. Panic crawled up my spine, hot and sharp, as my reckless past dueled with my imagined happy future.

The manic summer nights, the beach in Carenage, her tiny room with its creaky fan came rushing back. And now, while I was planning this whole life — America, my girlfriend, my future seemed to be disappearing.

On repeat, the singular solution looped again and again. I told myself, *If I could get to New York, I could earn enough to take care of them all, send money back, and make things right. Money will solve this.*

But when she looked at me, this woman's eyes saw through every hole in my proposal. Her stare made me feel I was trapped. Screwed. A kid myself at nineteen with this girl I'd pushed away, carrying my pickney…a child.

In the thick, humid air, a mosquito buzzed near my ear. I swatted at it absently, my hand missing its mark. It circled back, landing on my arm, biting before I could react.

The sting snapped me back to the moment—this moment that had me in a chokehold—and I dropped my arm to my side.

"Look," I said, my tone desperate. "I'll fix this. I'll break up with her. It's over already—I just need to tell her." The girl's expression didn't change, so I pressed on, the lies flowing easier with each word. "I'll marry you after the baby comes, okay? We'll do it right, build a life together. I'll take care of you. Both of you."

Her eyes softened a little.

She bit her lip, searching my face. I held out the promise I would not keep. I lied because I had no choice. *What else could I say to this girl?* I had to get her out of this house without any further ado. If I could survive the night, it would be okay. Once I got to America, I could make everything right.

"It will be happily ever after, for us," I whispered, though the words tasted bitter.

The mosquito buzzed again, a tiny witness to how my lies worked.

I drove her home, plastering on a smile. I avoided eye contact as my silver '58 Morris Minor crept backward from her house.

That evening was the night I met my daughter, growing in that girl's belly; and it was the last time I saw her mother.

* * *

Two hours later, I sat at the kitchen table across from my mother.

I felt an overwhelming need to claw my way back into the good graces of the most powerful lady in my world.

She stared at me, arms folded, her thick lips pressed into a thin line. It was well past her bedtime. Exhaustion showed in how her shoulders sagged, and her eyes lingered on mine, heavy with disappointment.

She was still in her blue mou mou with tiny white flowers—creased and wilted from being worn since morning, and she hadn't found a moment to change into her nightgown amidst the *commesse* raging in her yard. I knew she'd been arguing with my father earlier—probably about me, about this—because her face still carried the traces of frustration she couldn't quite mask.

"Are you going to tell me the truth now, or you still planning to play stupid?" she asked, voice quiet but sharp enough to cut.

I sighed, running a hand over my face. "I'm already engaged to her, Ma."

Her eyebrow lifted, unimpressed. "Which one?"

"My girlfriend, Margaret." The words felt heavier than I expected. "The wedding's in thirty days. We're leaving for America right after. I got my papers sorted."

I added in my mind, *"And once I'm there, I'll make enough money to take care of everyone, including the baby. It will all work out. I won't cause you any more trouble, Ma."*

My mother didn't flinch, didn't blink. But, in rapid succession, her questions came.

"And you are only now telling me about this wedding? You were going to run away and not tell your father or me?" Looking up to the ceiling, she bawled, "What kind of man I raise, Lord?

"So what about the child, then? What you planning to do with your flesh and blood? Leave it in the sun to bake?"

I looked down at the table, shame burning through my body, gurgling up into my throat. "Ma," I croaked, my voice cracking, "I'm not sure who that child father is."

The lie felt like acid in my mouth, but I clung to it like a lifeline.

My words hit the room like lightning. There was no mistaking their impact. My mother froze utterly still as if the whole house had been caught in the pause between the flash and the roar.

The quiet was absolute. Heavy. In it was a pledge of tyranny. Not even the fan dared to creak.

Then came the thunder.

"Boy, what kinda stupidness yuh talkin' about?" she started, Trini dialect rising in anger, her sing-song voice increasing to a crescendo at a dizzying tempo. "After all this *commesse* in my yard tonight? After all these tears, all this talking, all these lies you just finish telling that poor girl?" Her hands pounded the table, sending a small tin of sugar rattling to the edge.

"You out here bringing shame on this family, on yuh

father name, and for what? For you to turn around and tell me yuh ain't sure? You mean to tell me yuh let her walk in here, belly up, and yuh saying that child ain't yours?" Her voice cracked with fury, her accent thickening with every word.

She got up then, pacing the small kitchen, her mou mou swishing around her ankles as she pointed at me like she was lecturing a schoolroom full of misbehaving children.

"Yuh think this is a joke, eh? Yuh think life is one big fête? Well, let me tell yuh something, mister man — this is not about you no more. If that child come into this world and is yours, it doh matter what plans you have, what you think yuh doing with your life. You will step up." She leaned in, jabbing a finger toward my chest. "Yuh hear me? You will step up!"

I opened my mouth to respond, but nothing came out. In my mind, I was already across the ocean, making enough money to fix everything. Nothing I could say would make a difference, not now.

She sat down, threw her head back, and steadied her breathing for a few moments.

Finally, she shook her head, making a small, sharp motion. "You are my only son and I love you. And, you're a damn coward, boy," she muttered.

Then she stood, leaving me alone in the kitchen, guilt twisting my stomach into knots even as I thought, *I won't let this disrupt my plan to be a man. Once I get to America, I'll make it all right.*

** * **

With maniacal precision, I executed the blueprint I imagined my father would approve of.

I got married. It was a small, simple civil ceremony, with only my mother and father as witnesses. My new wife was overjoyed even though there was no celebration, no fanfare — just signatures and a few words to bind our futures together. When she smiled at me across the desk at the registry office, I saw salvation in her eyes. She wasn't just my escape route but my chance at redemption.

No one from her side of the family was there. Her father had left them when she was a child, and her mother and brother emigrated to the United States a few years later, leaving her behind at age twelve with an *Auntie* of no blood relation who already had a houseful of kids. She never really felt like she belonged in that home. By seventeen, she struck out on her own, determined to create her own sense of family. That fierce independence was one of the reasons I admired her so much right from the start.

Her steady presence felt like an anchor in my storm-tossed life. Where the other girl had been all raucous rhythm and uncertain tomorrows, my wife was sheet music perfectly composed. She believed in me in a way that made me want to be better; the man she saw when she looked at me. How she'd laid out our future — the trucking company, the house in Brooklyn, our weekend events in Long Island clubs for respectable Trini expats — made me feel like I could step into my father's definition of a man.

When she worked on my tourist immigration papers each evening, her face set in careful concentration, I'd watch her and think, *This woman will save me from myself.*

At the end of the rainy season, we left the island. I walked away from the girl who'd danced into my fête that night and our unborn baby, beginning a new life in New York City in the start of a brutal winter. I told myself it was temporary, that I'd soon make enough money to care for everyone. But as time went on, I understood these were just more lies I'd learned to live with, even as I tried to become the man my wife deserved.

Back home, things were different for the girl. She told my mother about her parents disowning and shunning her entirely for bringing shame to their name. A child out of wedlock was an unforgivable sin in their eyes.

"Humm." That was all I said in response to my mother's report. I offered no other response or solution. *I'll send money. I'll take care…*

As if she could hear my thoughts, my mother said, "I hope the tide don't turn, so you won't have to eat your words."

Chapter 4—Mary and Cecil

January 1970, Dry Season

Mary froze in the bedroom doorway, heart pounding as she saw Cecil hunched over the bed, meticulously sorting through passports, work permits, and letters from St. Croix—each a silent promise of the life they longed for. His reading glasses perched low on his nose as he squinted at the documents in the dim light of their bedside lamp.

"The processing fee going up next month," he said without looking up. "We need to send these papers soon if we want to catch this batch." His voice carried the weight of twenty-five years working heavy machinery at WASA, Trinidad's water and sewerage authority, of dreams deferred and opportunities missed.

Mary stood in the doorway, her hands still damp from washing the dishes. She watched her husband—a proud man who had worked every day since he was fourteen, who had built their home with his own hands, and who now saw St. Croix as their next chance at something better.

"Cecil," she said softly, "we need to talk about the girl."

His hands stilled over the papers. "Which girl?"

"You know which one." Mary moved into the room, settling on the edge of the bed. "The one carrying our grandchild."

Cecil's jaw tightened. "Joromi make his bed. Let him lie in it."

"And what about her? She just a child herself." Mary's voice was gentle but firm. "Her parents throw her out, Cecil. She have nowhere to go."

"And that's our problem?" But even as he said it, his voice lacked conviction. He removed his glasses, pinching the bridge of his nose. "Mary, this is our chance. Good money in St. Croix. Proper work. We could send something home for the boy too, help him sort himself out."

"The boy gone already," Mary said quietly. "Running to America with that woman, leaving this poor girl behind." She reached across the papers to take his hand. "But we still here."

Cecil looked at their joined hands – hers tough from years of domestic work, his rough and scarred from years of hard labor. When he spoke again, his voice was lower, uncertain. "What you asking me, Mary?"

"I am asking you to help me do what's right." She squeezed his hand. "That girl needs somebody to stand for her. And that baby…" She paused, letting the word hang between them. "That baby is going to be our blood."

"Mary…" There was a warning in his voice but also a plea. "We plan this move for three years. The green cards are ready. My cousin already find work for me with the construction company there."

"I know, love." She shifted closer, her free hand coming up to cup his cheek. "But some things more important than plans."

He leaned into her touch, eyes closing briefly. When he opened them again, they were filled with a mixture of resignation and admiration. "You planning to take that girl in, *ent*? Already make up your mind."

"She need a family now more than ever." Mary's thumb stroked his cheek. "And that baby going to need grandparents who know where they come from. Who know their stories, their roots."

Cecil was quiet for a long moment, looking at the papers scattered across their bed—all those dreams and plans reduced to official letterheads and government stamps. Finally, he gathered them up, straightening them into a neat pile.

"You know," he said, a hint of his usual gruffness returning, "my father used to say a man who don't listen to his wife does leave half his brain in the yard." He set the pile aside. "And you, woman, you always had more sense than me."

Mary's eyes filled with tears. "You not vex with me? For asking you to give up St. Croix?"

"Vex?" He pulled her close, pressing a kiss to her forehead. "How I could be vex with the woman who make me better than I am?" His voice grew thick. "Besides, you think I could leave you here? Go to St. Croix by myself like some bachelor boy?" He shook his head. "Nah. Where you go, I go. Where you stay, I stay."

Mary buried her face in his neck, breathing in the familiar scent of him – soap and tobacco and decades of shared life. "The money is going to be tight," she whispered.

"Money always tight," he said, stroking her back. "But family..." He paused, as if tasting the word. "Family worth more than money."

They sat together in the dim light, the papers forgotten, while the night insects sang their endless song outside their window. Tomorrow, they would begin the work of making room in their lives for a lost girl and an unborn child. Tomorrow, they would face the whispers of *macocious* neighbors and the judgment of friends. But tonight, they held each other, secure in the knowledge that sometimes the bravest thing you can do is stay where you're needed most.

"You too soft, woman," Cecil murmured into her hair, but his voice was full of love.

Mary smiled against his chest. "And you too hard, man. That's why God put us together. To balance things out."

Cecil chuckled, the sound rumbling through both of them. "Well then, best we stay that way." He pulled back to look at her, his expression growing serious. "But Mary…we going do this right. That girl going to finish school. And that baby…" His voice softened. "That baby going to know they come from people who stand up for what's right, even when it hard."

Mary nodded, her heart full. In the years to come, she would remember this night—not as the moment they gave up their dreams of St. Croix, but as the night they chose a different kind of future, one measured not in dollars and cents but in the currency of love and duty and the quiet strength it takes to stay.

"I wish Joromi had stayed."

"If wishes were horses, you would ride, woman."

Chapter 5—Joromi

March 1970, Spring

My mother, ever dutiful, took over in the girl's parents' place—and, well...my place.

I didn't expect this from her. Each time she called, her voice carried a weight. She'd tell me about doctor's visits, about buying baby clothes, about holding the girl's hand through morning sickness. My mother—who I'd only ever known to be poised and reserved—had become this girl's champion.

"She need somebody," my mother would say, her voice thick with meaning. "Since everybody else turn their back on her."

The accusation in those words hit hard. I'd try to change the subject, ask about anything else, but my mother wouldn't let me escape.

"The baby kick today," she'd say, or "The doctor say everything looking good."

Each update reminded me of what I was running from, of the life growing back home while I played at being a different man in New York. Sometimes, as I commuted home from work, alone, I'd catch myself wondering about them both—the girl and the baby she carried. In those moments, the tendrils of my choices encircled my throat until I could barely breathe.

My mother was there when my child was born.

"She's the spitting image of you." The words crackled through the phone line, my mother's voice rising to a shout as always. She believed the physical distance between us demanded volume, but this time, I heard something else in her tone—pride, joy, and, beneath it all, a challenge. "She have your eyes, your nose, even the little dimple in her chin."

Each detail hit like a hammer to my carefully constructed wall of denial. It was my daughter. My child. The reality I'd been trying so hard to escape was wearing my face.

I barely had time to process this when my mother's voice changed, dropping to a solemn tone, but still loud. "Son, the girl, she passed away."

The words didn't make sense at first. They floated in the air like smoke, formless and impossible to grasp. "Wh— what?" My voice cracked, betraying emotions I didn't know I still had for the girl.

"She didn't make it. She gave birth to a healthy baby girl but…complications, they said."

The world tilted sideways. The kitchen around me blurred and shifted like I was seeing it through water. Sounds became distant and distorted—the voice of Tyrone Davis on the radio ironically singing, "Turn Back the Hands of Time," the tick of the clock, my wife's voice asking if I was okay—all of it warped and twisted like a badly tuned radio. My ears rang with a high-pitched whine from inside my own head.

The pain hit in waves. First, a sharp stab beneath my ribs made me gasp. Then, a deeper irritation spread over my skin, a feeling of a layer ripping as if something essential was being torn away. My heart caved in on itself; each beat, a struggle against the void opening up inside me. The hollow feeling spread until I could feel it in my bones, in the spaces between my fingers, in the air in my lungs.

My hands trembled as I grasped the edge of the kitchen counter. The cool Formica under my palms was the only thing that felt real. When my knees finally gave out, I sank to the floor, the cold tiles pressing against my legs through my thin pants.

My wife stood frozen a few feet away, her lips parted in surprise. In our life together, she'd never seen me like this—never seen the facade crack, never witnessed the rawness beneath. And now here I was, breaking apart on our kitchen floor.

"You're gone?" I muttered, the words coming out choked and strange. I wasn't sure who I was talking to—the girl whose laugh used to light up rooms, whose touch used to make my skin burn, whose love I'd been too young and stupid to recognize for what it was? The truth hit me then—I had loved her. Beneath all my father's warnings and my own fears, despite everything I'd told myself about being practical and responsible, I had loved her wildly, completely. And I'd thrown it away.

The shame crashed over me like a wave, hot and suffocating. This wasn't just about not being there for the birth or deserting her to face judgment alone. This was about denying the depth of what we'd had, about letting my father's voice in my head drown out the voice in my heart. I had failed her in every possible way—failed to love her enough when she was here, failed to stand by her when she needed me, failed even to acknowledge the truth of what she meant to me; and now it was too late.

She had faced everything alone—I imagined the whispers, the stares, the rejection of her family—while I aspired to be the man my father wanted me to be. She had carried our child, endured the pain of birth, and died without me ever telling her that what we had was real, that she wasn't just some summer fling I needed to outgrow.

My wife picked up the phone receiver I'd dropped, only to hear my mother shriek, "We named the baby after her mother. When are you coming for Trisha?"

* * *

"So, what now? You think I'm going to raise that girl's child?" Her voice was sharp, as her eyes narrowed, and she looked down at me in a way that slashed straight through me.

"Maggie, she's a baby," I said softly, almost pleading. "An innocent baby who didn't ask for any of this."

"And neither did I!" Her arms crossed tightly over her chest, her stance firm and unyielding. "You promised me — promised me— this wasn't your child."

I did swear this to Margaret. I said it so confidently back then because I wanted to believe it.

"I thought...I thought she wasn't. But now —"

"Now, what?" she snapped, her voice rising, interrupting me. "Now you've changed your mind? After keeping quiet all this time? You didn't even have the decency to talk to me about it! You knew your mother was taking care of her!"

She was right about that. I'd buried it, pushed it aside like it would solve itself. But it didn't.

"What do you want me to s—say, Maggie?" My voice faltered, but I pressed on, trying to find some ground to stand on. "That I'm sorry? Fine. I'm sorry. I'm sorry for what this means, for what it does to us. But that little girl —"

"No!" Her voice splintered with emotion as she interrupted again. "Don't you dare try to guilt me! This isn't my fault, and a baby by another woman is not my responsibility. I married a single man. A man with no kids!"

She was right. This wasn't her fault. It was mine. It had always been mine.

Silence hung heavy for an uncomfortable minute. She broke it.

"Our immigration application papers did not mention a child. We can't change it; otherwise, they become void." Pausing for only a fraction of a breath, she asked, "She has her mother's name, but does she have yours?"

I did not answer her question about the baby's last name but said, "She has no one. Her mother's gone. The girl's parents won't own the baby."

My voice was quieter now, desperate but fading. "What do you want me to do, leave her to the system?"

"I don't care what you do." Her words came cold, final, as she shook her head. "But I'm telling you now — I will not raise another woman's child. Not now. Not ever!"

And there it was. Her last word. I knew it was coming, but the punch of her statement made me wince. My wife, the woman I'd chosen, stood her ground firmly while I felt mine crumbling beneath me.

"Fine." The word barely came out, weighted with resignation. "I'll ask my mother to take her. She'll… she'll do what I can't."

"Do what you need to do." Maggie's tone chilled, and her distance from me was expansive when she ended the conversation by stating, "Just don't bring her into this house."

I sat on the cold tile floor of our apartment's kitchen, slumping my shoulders and holding my head as I tried to make sense of everything. The practical voice in my mind — the one that sounded so much like my father — kept laying out the facts: *A stable life in America meant opportunities, and opportunities meant money. Money meant I could provide for everyone — my wife, my mother, and, yes, my daughter.*

This marriage and this move to America were bringing me stability — real stability, the kind my father always preached about, the kind that meant something. In New York I was becoming somebody — even after just a few months. I was making good money. From here, I could give my daughter a good life — better schools, better chances, better everything, even if she was not physically here with me.

The truth of our situation was that I couldn't jeopardize this chance. Not now. If I claimed Trisha as mine, added her on the immigration papers, everything would fall apart. We'd lose our shot at life in America. Then what could I offer her? What kind of father could I be, stuck on the island, struggling to make ends meet with my parties and odd jobs?

No. Better to establish myself first. Get settled. Build something solid. I could provide for her from here — send money, make sure she had everything. My mother would raise her right, give her the love and guidance she required until I could do more. *This isn't abandonment,* I told myself. It was strategy. Planning. Being smart about it.

But I would have to deny her my name and my presence. *For now. Just for now.*

"It's only for a little while. I'll get to you soon," I whispered the promise, the words tasting like hope and lies mixed together. I believed it, though — I had to believe it. This was the responsible thing to do. The grown-up thing.

This was me, making the hard choices for the greater good.

Deep inside, a smaller voice tried to speak up, questioning, *Am I finding a way to escape my responsibilities?* But I pushed it down, buried it under layers of practicality and pledges. I would make this right. At least, I believed economic security was the answer—what I needed to give and what Trisha wanted. Soon, I could provide that— eventually, I would have something to offer when I become a citizen.

I didn't know then that "eventually" would stretch into years and "soon" would become one of the heaviest words in my vocabulary.

Chapter 6—Margaret

March 1970, Spring

The moment Joromi's knees hit the cold kitchen tiles, clutching the edge of the counter like a lifeline, I knew something really horrible was happening. His anguished voice filled the room, a low guttural cry that shattered the air like glass breaking. The words, *"She's gone,"* escaped his lips, broken and trembling, as if speaking them made it real.

I stood there, frozen. My arms wrapped tightly around myself as if I could shield my heart from the storm raging in him. I should have felt pity, compassion even. But all I felt was anger—hot, sharp, and bitter. Anger at her, at him, at the fragile life that connected them both and had now entangled itself in mine.

"She's dead, Maggie," Joromi said again, his voice

cracking. "She's gone…"

I couldn't take it. The way his shoulders shook, the way his grief filled the room like an aberration. Grief for a woman who wasn't me, who had left behind a child I never asked for—that HE never asked for, who would now haunt my marriage in ways I couldn't escape.

I had to end it. I had to make it clear. My words came sharp and cold, lancing his pain. "Just don't bring her into this house."

His head snapped up, his freshly tear-streaked face staring at me in disbelief, but I didn't stay to continue watching his reaction. I turned and walked out of the kitchen, my steps firm, deliberate. Once in the bedroom, I slammed the door shut and locked it. My hands were trembling as I reached for the phone and dialed.

It rang twice before Avrielle answered. "Hello?"

"It's him," I said, my voice shaking with barely contained fury. "It's Joromi. I can't believe this, Avrielle. He's crying over her. The mother of that baby."

She was quiet for a moment. "Wait. The baby is born? Whoa! Are you saying he's still hung up on the mother?"

"Yes!" I snapped, pacing the room. The phone cord twisted around my fingers and body as I walked. "And now, with her gone—"

"Wait, gone? What do you mean?"

"The woman died giving birth," I updated my friend and kept on going. "Now he wants to take in that baby. He actually expects me to raise her child! Can you imagine?"

Avrielle sighed. "Maggie, it's not the child's fault."

"I know that!" The words came out harsher than I intended. I stopped pacing and took a deep breath. "But what about me, Avrielle? What about our life? We've only been in America five months, and our green cards aren't even final yet. If this gets out, if anyone questions our situation… it's too risky. I can't do it."

"Maggie," Avrielle said gently, "you don't have to do anything you're not ready for. But are you sure this isn't about more than just the risk of deportation?"

"It is," I admitted, sinking onto the edge of the bed. "It's about her. I feel like I've been competing with her memory since I met him. And now, even in death, she's still here. She still has a claim on him."

"You're allowed to feel that way," she said. "You're human. But Maggie, you need to figure out what you can live with. Can you stay with Joromi knowing he's tied to her forever? Or…"

I closed my eyes, letting the weight of her unsaid words settle over me. "I don't know," I whispered. "But I know I can't pretend this isn't tearing me apart."

There was silence on the other end of the line for a while before Avrielle spoke again. "Whatever you decide, Maggie, make sure it's for you. Not for him, not for anyone else."

I hung up the phone and sat in the stillness of the bedroom, my mind racing. The woman was gone, yes, but her ghost lingered. And that baby — her baby — was a living reminder of everything I wanted to forget.

I pressed my back against the door and slid to the floor, my tears spilling freely. *He can't bring that child into this house,* I told myself again, the words a mantra I clung to.

The practical side of my brain took over. Our green cards weren't final. One mistake, one raised eyebrow from an immigration officer, and everything we'd worked for could fall apart. Joromi and I had left everything behind for this chance, and I wouldn't let it be ruined. Not for this.

Then I thought, *Separate the finances!*

Yes, I'd make sure of this. If Joromi wanted to send money back to Trinidad, it wouldn't come from my account. I wouldn't see it or feel it, and I certainly wouldn't be part of raising that child.

I was so focused on protecting what Joromi and I had built that I couldn't see the irony of this situation. In refusing to acknowledge his baby, I was re-creating the very abandonment I'd experienced as a young girl.

My mother had left me in Trinidad to chase dreams in America with a new man, leaving me to be raised by the neighborhood Auntie. I grew up watching the front door, waiting for letters that came less and less frequently, for promises of visits that never materialized. Each birthday, each Christmas, the space where my mother should have been grew larger.

"Don't depend on nobody, depend on yourself!" the Auntie would tell me as she taught me how to braid my hair each weekend. The words became my armor, my shield against hurt. I built my life around being independent, around never needing anyone so completely that they could dump and destroy me as my father had done and then my mother.

Joromi had been the only exception to my rule.

In him, I saw someone I could trust with my carefully assembled life—someone who seemed to want the same things I did: stability, structure, a life built on solid ground rather than shifting sands. When he looked at me with those eyes that held such determination to be better, to be more, I let myself believe in something bigger than my autonomy.

But love, I was learning, was more complicated than the neat boxes I tried to put it in. Even as Joromi started building this life with me in New York, I knew part of him remained tethered to Trinidad—to a past he couldn't fully leave behind, to a newborn daughter whose existence challenged everything I thought we were building together. Thoughts inflamed my mind like an out-of-control wildfire.

Margaret, you spent your life avoiding dependence, yet here you are, choosing to love a man you not only need but apparently are desperately clinging to.

Does he think I will financially support this situation? He's crazy!

Or worse, will Joromi insist I care for and love that woman's baby? No way!

Will he leave me here and return to this bastard child?

* * *

I would later understand that that night, I could not, would not, see how my actions stood between the child and her father. I would make Joromi separate himself from his kid, just as my father and mother had done to me. Each time Joromi mentioned sending money to Trinidad, each time he got quiet after those phone calls with his mother, I felt my carefully constructed world trembling.

Maybe that was why the thought of Joromi supporting another woman's child made my stomach churn from the beginning. It felt like a betrayal—not just of me, but of everything I'd worked so hard to escape. I had clawed my way to stability and sacrificed so much to get here without the support from my parent living abroad— I was the forsaken girl, and now I begrudged the attention that my husband gave to the child he left behind.

I couldn't see that my fear of losing what I had was making me perpetuate a cycle that had devastated me. Not yet.

I would come to understand that sometimes, the most challenging reflections to face are the ones that show us what we've become. But eventually, I did begin to see. Eventually, I began to heal and open up.

Chapter 7—Margaret

June 1973, Summer

It surprised me how much things had changed in three years. I hadn't expected our marriage to feel so solid, so full of love, after everything we'd been through. Joromi and I had found a rhythm, a quiet understanding that softened the sharp edges of the past.

He was different now—more grounded, more present. The Joromi who once held everything inside now shared pieces of himself more freely, and I found myself drawn to him in ways I hadn't imagined.

One evening, as we sat together on the couch after dinner, his arm draped lazily around my shoulders, he spoke about her again.

"Trisha started school this year," he said, his voice

soft, almost wistful. "Ma says she's smart. Always asking questions, always curious." He chuckled. "Apparently, she loves red. Like me."

I leaned into him, resting my head on his chest. "She sounds like a bright little girl."

He nodded, his hand absently tracing circles on my arm. "She is. Ma says she reminds her of me at that age — full of energy, always running around, getting into trouble."

There was no guardedness in his voice now when he spoke of Trisha, no hesitation. Over time, he had learned to share these moments with me, and I had learned to listen. It wasn't always easy — sometimes, the ghost of my jealousy for his first love, Trisha's mother, still whispered in my ear in a breathy tease, *I'll always be his soulmate* — but I knew that was my insecurity. I push that voice down and away, willing myself to believe *He loves ME and needs me. It's okay if he also loves his daughter, he needs to talk about her so she's present in his life. It has nothing to do with the girl's mother.*

"Do you miss her?" I asked, surprising even myself with the question. I told myself that the "her" was his daughter, not the baby's mother. But I held my breath until he answered.

He was quiet for a moment. "Every day," he admitted. "But I also know she's in good hands. Ma loves her. She's giving Trisha a life full of stability, tradition, family. Things I can't give her right now."

I reached for his hand, intertwining my fingers with his. "You're doing what you can, Joromi. You're giving her a chance at a better life. That counts for something."

He squeezed my hand, his eyes meeting mine. "You think so?"

"I know so," I said, my voice firm. "You didn't walk away from her. You made sure she had everything she needed. That's more than most would do." The images of my father and mother were foremost in my mind when I said this.

Joromi pulled me closer, pressing a kiss to my forehead. "You're too good to me, Maggie. I don't deserve you."

I smiled, brushing my thumb against his jawline. "Maybe not," I teased, "but you're stuck with me now."

We laughed together, the sound filling the small apartment. In moments like this, I felt the depth of our love, the quiet strength that had grown between us over the years. I caught him staring at me, a curious smile playing on his lips.

"What?" I asked, raising an eyebrow.

"Nothing," he said, shaking his head. "I just…I love this version of us. I didn't think we'd get here, but we did."

The intimacy of his voice calmed me, and the feeling captured my breath. I reached for Joromi's hand, my fingers slipping over his calloused palm, still rough from the hours he spent hauling crates at the dock. We initially planned for him to work with my brother, but it demanded continual travel and would have kept him away too often. Instead, he chose a steady union job at the ports that allowed me to welcome him home every evening. But it meant I had to work too; I did not mind. His thumb grazed against the back of my hand, his touch familiar yet electric. Whenever he touched me like this, even after all these years, sparks of delight popped off in my brain, and my body warmed and perked up, ever ready.

I love this man so much.

"We worked for this." I looked up at him. My voice came out soft and steady, which belied my inner excitement. "And it is worth it."

Joromi's lips curved into a slow, deliberate smile that showed off his gorgeous teeth and made his already chiseled, dimpled jawline even more defined. His copper-toned skin gleamed in the soft light of our apartment, the sweat of the day lingering on him in a way that somehow added to his appeal. At six-foot-three, he towered over me even when we sat side by side on the couch, his muscular frame exuding an effortless strength. He leaned back slightly, his arm moving to casually rest along the top of the cushion, his broad shoulders stretching the thin cotton of his T-shirt.

Could he read how I responded to him?

"Yeah, Maggie," he said, his deep voice carrying a hint of that lilting Trini accent that made my name sound like music. "We really did."

I smiled, shaking my head slightly, letting my curls bounce. I was growing my hair out and it hung around my shoulders. "I didn't think we'd get here," I admitted, my voice trailing off as I caught his gaze.

His eyes softened, their dark brown depths holding steady on me. "You had doubts?" he teased, tilting his head slightly. The movement was playful, but his tone was sincere.

"Plenty," I said, with a small laugh, smoothing down the hem of my floral house dress. The soft cotton clung to my curves, and I caught the way his eyes flicked to the swell of my hips before meeting mine again. "But here we are."

He shifted closer, his arm squeezing my shoulder. The warmth of his touch grounded me, but it was his gaze that held me still. "You're more beautiful now than the day I met you, Maggie," he murmured, his eyes tracing my face as if memorizing it. "You know that?"

I felt my cheeks burning. "Lord, have mercy! Stop, you're making me blush."

"Good," he said, leaning in just slightly, his eyes never leaving mine. "You're even prettier when you blush."

I rolled my eyes, but the corners of my mouth betrayed me with a smile. "Charm won't get you out of dishes tonight."

He laughed. Its deep, rich sound filled the entire room. His hand slid down from my shoulder, resting on my waist, where his thumb traced slow circles through the fabric. "Worth a try," he said, his voice low, the teasing note unmistakable.

I leaned into him, resting my head against his chest, the steady beat of his heart thrumming under my ear. His arm tightened around me protectively, his other hand brushing the curls from my temple.

I closed my eyes briefly, letting the silence settle around us. It wasn't the uneasy quiet of years ago, filled with unsaid words and jagged edges. This was something more peaceful, warmer — a place where we could simply be.

"You're different now, Joromi," I said after a while. "More open."

His hand stilled on my waist momentarily before resuming its slow, soothing movement. "You make it easy, Maggie," he said, pressing his lips to my forehead again. "You make everything easier."

My laughter bubbled out before I could stop it. "Says the man who drives me mad every other day."

He pulled back slightly, tilting my chin with a finger so I could meet his gaze. "And you still love me," he said, his smile softening into something that made my heart race at a scary pace.

I swatted his hand playfully, but my own smile mirrored his. "Don't let it go to your head," I said, resting my palm on his chest. The muscles beneath my touch tensed slightly as he adjusted his posture, his body heat radiating through the thin barrier of fabric.

He was silent for a moment, studying. Finally, he said, "You've always been my soft place to land, Maggie. Even when I didn't deserve it."

I kissed his jawline, lingering long enough to feel the stubble graze my lips. "We're stronger together, Joromi," I whispered.

"Then, let's do the dishes together, nah?"

Shaking my head and joining his laughter, I said, "You are something else, Joromi Enoch!"

"Only for you, Margaret Enoch."

* * *

Later that evening, when I swayed slightly as I rose to turn off the bedside lamp, he was at my side in an instant, his hands on my waist.

"Maggie, you alright?" His brow furrowed, his voice laced with concern.

"I'm fine," I said, though the slight wave of dizziness made me grip his arm for balance. "I've just been feeling off lately. Nauseous, tired…"

He stilled, his hands warm and steady. "Maggie…" His voice trailed off, his eyes narrowing slightly as he studied me, looking at my midsection. "Could it be…?"

The realization struck us both at the same time. My hands flew to my stomach, my breath catching. "Joromi, I might be pregnant."

For a moment, the world seemed to wobble, the air thick with the weight of what I'd just said. Then, slowly, his face broke into the most radiant smile I'd ever seen. "You're serious?" he whispered, his voice barely audible.

I nodded, tears spilling over as I met his gaze. "I think so."

He laughed—a sound so full of joy that it felt like

music. Wrapping me in his arms, he held me tightly, his head resting against mine. "Maggie," he murmured, his voice dense with emotion. "Are we going to have a baby?"

And just like that, the future we'd worked so hard to build stretched bright and full before us.

Just then, the memory surfaced—the night I was with him when Trisha's mom revealed he would be a father. His face had crumpled under the weight of the news, eyes wide with fear, his breaths uneven as if the very air around him had turned heavy. But now, as his hand rested gently on my stomach, his eyes shone with a light so pure it made my chest ache. A smile tugged at his lips, unrestrained and unguarded, and I couldn't help but revel in the transformation. My man, so full of joy, was brimming with love at the thought of a child we had created together.

I suppose the passage of our years of marriage, the closeness we now shared, and, if I'm being honest, the hormones of pregnancy made what I said next surprise even me.

I placed my hand over his, feeling the strength that had carried us through so much. "Joromi," I began, my voice steady but soft, "now that we're legal immigrants, I think it's time. After this baby comes, let's go and meet Trisha."

He looked at me, his eyes wide with surprise and something deeper—relief, maybe.

"She should know us," I continued, summoning courage, "and her sibling. It's important, Joromi. We've built this life together, and I think it's time to open the door for her to be a part of it."

He didn't speak for a long moment, his gaze searching mine as if trying to be sure I truly meant it. Then, slowly, his lips curved into a grateful smile. "You really mean that Maggie?"

My head nodded slowly under the weight of my spirit's decision.

But a moment later, a terrifying darkness descended, and I felt like I'd plunged into an icy river. My arms flailed until two strong hands gripped my shoulders, steadying me. A voice—her voice—murmured dreamily, *"Ah know yuh feel de pinch from meh memory, but motherhood tie we together now. Ah ent have no bad mind fuh yuh—only wishin' yuh find de kinda peace ah never did."*

When I came to, Joromi was still clutching my shoulders in panic. "Maggie, Maggie—wake up!"

I blinked and sat up, a gentle peace settling in my heart.

"I'm okay, Joromi. And yes," I said firmly. "It's time to see Trisha."

Chapter 8—Joromi

July 1975, Rainy Season

"What's your favorite color?"

Seriously? That was the best I could come up with. What kind of lame-ass question is that to ask your child the first time you meet her? Five years. It had taken me five years to meet Trisha in person finally.

At first, I couldn't leave America—the terms of my visa application meant any departure might prevent my return. Maggie constantly reminded me of this; her voice strained with barely concealed relief.

I threw myself into work, into building the life I thought I was supposed to want. The days bled into weeks, months, and years. I spoke with my mother as regularly as I could afford the international calls, drinking in every detail about Trisha. "She is walking now," my mother would say, or "She started school this week," or "Lord, this child smart like anything." Each milestone I missed sat like stones in my stomach.

Three years in, Maggie became pregnant. When Heather was born, the guilt nearly crushed me. Here I was, playing devoted father to one daughter while another grew up without me across an ocean. Before suggesting we visit Trinidad with Heather, Maggie never spoke of Trisha, as if my first child's existence might contaminate our carefully constructed American life. Even now, she sat stiffly in my mother's gallery, bouncing Heather on her knee, her eyes darting everywhere except toward Trisha.

Now, finally, face-to-face with my daughter, I, too, actively avoided eye contact. I had to. My mom said this girl looked like me when she was born. But, every time I looked at her, I saw the woman who delivered her to this world before stepping into her next life. *My heart softened when you said red was your favorite color, Trisha. Did you know it was your mother's favorite color? Did you know it was mine, too?*

I shoveled mouthfuls of the delicious meal my mother made me. She'd prepared all my favorites - her famous macaroni pie, callaloo, and even curried Cascadura fish that I'd never much cared for. But I made a show of tearing through its crispy flesh before pushing the well-seasoned river fish around my plate.

All the while, I was conscious of the little girl's eyes on me, occasionally drifting to her baby sister with undisguised curiosity. Heather, not yet understanding the weight of the moment, reached out toward Trisha with a toddler's innocent delight. I felt so much shame.

What should I say? What I wanted to say sat at the base of my throat. *You're coming home with me, Trisha. I want you to be with me.* But I knew those words were a fantasy I could never make real.

Maggie's tense shoulders and careful silence told me everything I needed to know. She was only open to my first daughter visiting—but living with us; not yet. So, I chewed up the unspoken words with the macaroni pie and swallowed them with the sorrel drink. It was then that I committed myself to being done with lying. *I will not lie to you, my daughter. I will remain silent instead.*

As I left for the hotel we had booked, I looked out the car window at my child. My voice came out steady, though my heart cracked with every word I said. "Trisha, will you be a good girl for your grandmother?"

Because I knew—deep down, without question, that leaving her with my mother meant giving Trisha something I couldn't: a home where she was treasured, not endured. She could grow up surrounded by unconditional love and not navigate the complicated waters of being an unwanted reminder. My mother had become more than just her grandmother; she was Trisha's fierce protector, her constant champion. In my mother's house, Trisha would never question her place or her worth. It wasn't about choosing the easier path for myself—it was about choosing the better route for my daughter.

As I drove the red rental car away from my childhood home, Heather sleeping in the back seat and Maggie's hand resting lightly on my arm, the final glimpse of a smiling Trisha in the rearview mirror branded itself onto my heart.

Even though I knew I was offering her an unshakeable foundation of love with my parents, I felt the ache of leaving. A silent question roared in my mind, *Would Trisha one day understand why I had to go? Would she forgive me for giving her sister the attention she will never know?*

* * *

Heather slept in Maggie's arms as we waited in Piarco's departure lounge. The American Airlines flight was delayed—something about mechanical issues in San Juan, Puerto Rico—leaving us stranded in this liminal space between my two lives.

A group of American tourists sprawled across the seats nearby, their sunburned faces and duty-free bags marking them as distinctly as their loud voices. They'd probably spent their week at the Hilton like us, venturing out only for carefully curated island tours. Behind them, a grandmother fussed over three small children while their parents sorted through passports and boarding passes.

"Your father pulled you aside before we left," Maggie said carefully, her free hand smoothing Heather's curls. "What did he say?"

I shifted in the hard plastic chair, remembering how my dad had cornered me in the kitchen while the women said their goodbyes. His voice had been gruff but carried an undertone I'd rarely heard before—something like understanding mixed with reproach and sadness.

"He spoke about Trisha," I admitted, watching

Maggie's shoulders tense slightly. "Said I was making a mistake trying to solve everything with money and distance. But…"

Maggie's hand stilled on Heather's head. "But?"

"But then he said something strange." I glanced at a young couple near the window, probably newlyweds heading home after their honeymoon, still wrapped in that bubble of early love. "He said maybe it's better this way. That my mother needs Trisha, that the girl gives her purpose."

What I didn't tell Maggie was the rest of it—how my father's eyes had grown distant as he spoke about stepparents and divided loyalties. "Some children need solid ground," he'd said, his meaning clear. "Better a grandmother's undivided love than a stepmother's reluctant tolerance."

I watched relief wash over Maggie's face, subtle but unmistakable. I knew what my wife needed to hear. Her shoulders relaxed, and she drew Heather closer, kissing our daughter's forehead.

"Your mother does dote on her," she offered, her tone softer now. "And Trisha seems… happy there."

Happy. I thought about Trisha's smile when she'd shown me her school books, her easy laughter with my mother, and the way she moved through that house as if nowhere else felt more like home. *Maybe she was happy.* But my heart told me I saw longing in my daughter's stares.

The departure board flickered, updating our delayed time yet again. Heather stirred in Maggie's arms, making those small sounds that meant she'd soon wake hungry and cranky. A stewardess in a crisp American Airlines uniform walked past, her heels clicking against the floor as she answered questions about the delay. Just another hour, and we'd be on our way back to New York, back to our carefully curated life where Trisha existed only in monthly phone calls and carefully worded letters.

"Your father's probably right," Maggie said, but she wasn't looking at me. "Some things are better left as they are."

I said nothing in response.

Across the lounge, a man about my age sat alone, staring at a photograph he kept turning over in his hands. I wondered what story he carried, what pieces of himself he was leaving behind on this island.

Maggie interrupted my people-watching, saying, "Your mother pulled me aside, too."

Surprised, I tensed and looked over at her, waiting.

"She wanted to make sure I understood my place." Maggie kept her eyes on Heather, smoothing our daughter's curls with practiced strokes. "She made it very clear that Trisha belongs in Trinidad, with her."

"What exactly did she say?"

"Oh, you know your mother." With a small, brittle laugh, Maggie mimicked my mother's manner of speaking. "*'That child needs stability. Not some new family trying to make space for her.'* Then she looked at Heather and said something about how some gardens can't handle transplanted flowers."

The airport's air conditioning felt suddenly colder. My mother's words, filtered through Maggie's voice, carried all the sharp edges of a cutlass.

"She's right, you know." Maggie's tone was almost sympathetic. "Trisha has her life there. Her school, her friends. Your mother…" She paused, choosing her words carefully. "Your mother has built her whole world around that child. It would be cruel to disrupt that now."

I watched a young family at the check-in counter, parents juggling passports and crying children. "I wasn't planning to—"

"I know," Maggie cut in quickly. "I just wanted you to know that your mother and I agree on this. Trisha stays where she belongs. Where she's happy."

There was that word again. Everyone seemed to think Trisha was happy. *Happy without me?*

The flight delay announcement crackled over the speakers again, but I barely heard it. My mother's strategy was clear—she'd found an ally in Maggie, using their mutual interests to ensure Trisha remained firmly under her care. And perhaps they were both right—my daughter did seem happy, rooted in the island soil my mother had so carefully tended.

"Flight 223 to New York-JFK, now boarding at Gate 3…"

As we gathered our things, I thought about what my father hadn't said, about the knowing look in his eyes when he spoke of my mother needing Trisha. Maybe he understood something I was only beginning to grasp—

sometimes, love means letting go, even when every instinct screams to hold on.

From my middle seat, I leaned past Maggie with Heather sleeping in her lap to peer through the plane's tiny window. The Northern Range rose majestic and green against the sky, and for a moment, I let myself wonder, *Trinity mountains, are you calling….?*

As the first heavy drops struck the window, that sweet idea of Trinidad being home for me dissolved. Rain quickly gathered into a shimmering sheet that blotted out the mountains. By the time the plane pushed back from the gate, the peaks had vanished behind nature's curtain—a conclusion more final than any words from Maggie, my father, or my mother could ever express.

Part Two

Growing Season

Scarlet Ibis James

Chapter 9—Trisha

July 1975, Rainy Season

The day my father came to visit, Granny insisted we cook Cascadura. I watched her in the kitchen that morning. Even though I was tall, my chin barely reached the counter as she cleaned the freshly caught fish, explaining each step with the patience of a woman who believed cooking was more than just feeding bodies — it was feeding souls.

"Look at the pretty scales," Granny said, holding up the fish so the sun coming through our window could make it sparkle. "See how they shine like tiny mirrors? That means it's a good one."

I couldn't stop staring at all the rainbow colors dancing on the fish. Even after it came out of the water, it was still so pretty! Granny said Cascadura isn't like the fish we get at the market – it's magic.

"You know what they say about Cascadura?" Granny asked in her special story-telling voice that always made me excited. "If you eat it, you have to come back to Trinidad before you die. No matter how far away you go, the island will call you home." She stopped cleaning the fish and looked at me with a secret glimmering in her eyes. "That's why we're making it today, you see?"

This was my earliest memory. I understood, even at five, that she meant it for him—my father who lived across the ocean in America. Maybe if he ate our Cascadura, the magic would work, and he'd come back to stay.

The kitchen filled with the scent of curry and garlic as she seasoned the fish, showing me how to crush the *chadon beni* leaves just so, releasing their sharp smell. "Your mother loved this dish," she said softly, and my hands stilled on the leaves. Granny didn't often speak of my mother, but when she did, it was always in the kitchen, as if the act of cooking loosened memories she usually kept tucked away.

Why did my father leave us, I wondered. He and his family had been in Trinidad for a few days already, but my grandfather said they were doing some sightseeing first. The tone of this declaration was rough, unusual. He punctuated the statement with a long, irreverent *steups* that made me giggle. I was never allowed to express myself with that sucking sound, so I looked towards my Granny to see if doing so got my grandfather in trouble. But she did not pay him any mind. She just continued her feverish preparations.

"Is he coming for me today, Granny?"

She did not answer me either. Her eyes were glued to the fish. I followed her gaze and cast my hopes into the flesh of the fish she was carefully scaling. Each knife scrape against its tough scales echoed in the quiet kitchen, louder than the thoughts tumbling in my mind.

The fish didn't flinch or resist—just lay there, accepting the inevitable. My young mind did not understand the animal was no longer alive; it contained magic, after all. Instead, I wondered if that was how I was supposed to feel.

I kept watching the front door, waiting and waiting. My tummy felt all jumpy with butterflies. When he finally came, his voice was so big it made me shake a little inside and out.

"What's your favorite color?" he asked me.

I peeked up at him through my curls and giggled shy-like. "Red," I said, hoping he'd smile real big. But his eyes didn't stay on me for long. They kept moving around, looking at Granny, his plate, and everywhere except me.

He ate the Cascadura fish so fast, like he was really, really hungry. He tore through the crispy outside part to get to the soft inside, then ate up all the macaroni pie with the callaloo. I wanted him to see the pretty napkins I'd put out and the red hibiscus flower I found special for him, but he was too busy talking and laughing with Granny.

When he finished eating, my grandfather pulled him into the backyard. I watched them talking until Granny called me, making me jump.

"Trisha! Stop being *macocious*! Go and spend some

time with your sister!"

My sister. I had no idea I had one until today. I reluctantly padded off from the back to the front of the house, where my father's wife sat in the gallery in our Adirondack chairs. My sister was perched on her lap, all soft brown curls and big eyes, wearing a frilly yellow dress that looked like it belonged in a fancy shop window.

I hung back near the doorway, my hands twisting in the hem of my pink play dress. Granny had tried to change me into something nicer, but I'd refused.

"Come here, Trisha," my father's wife said, her voice gentle but firm, like a teacher's. "This is Heather. She's been very excited to meet her big sister."

Heather stared at me with wide eyes, her thumb stuck firmly in her mouth. She looked nothing like me — her skin was lighter; her hair fell in neat ringlets instead of wild coils like mine. But something in the shape of her eyes reminded me of the man who'd just asked me my favorite color in the kitchen.

"Hi," I whispered, not moving closer. My bare feet felt glued to the cool concrete floor.

"She's shy," my father's wife — Miss Margaret, Granny had said to call her — explained to Heather. "Just like you sometimes are with new people."

Of course, I was not shy. But, I was not sure what I was supposed to be feeling towards these strangers at that moment.

Miss Margaret bounced Heather on her knee, making the little girl giggle around her thumb. That laugh loosened something in my chest. Before I knew what I was doing, I'd taken a step forward. "I have a doll," I said suddenly. "Want to see?"

Heather's eyes lit up, and she nodded, pulling her thumb out of her mouth. "Dolly?"

I ran to get my favorite doll, the one Granny had made me with brown skin and yarn hair just like mine. When I came back, Heather had slipped off Margaret's lap and was waiting expectantly.

"Her name is Ruby," I said, holding out the doll. "Because red is my favorite color."

"Dada wed! Me wed too!" with grabby hands reaching for Ruby, mispronouncing my color.

I felt my breath catch. There it was — another piece of him I shared. I watched as Heather hugged Ruby close.

I could feel Miss Margaret watching us. "She has other dolls at home," she said quietly. "But I think she likes yours, Trisha."

I wanted to snatch Ruby back, to say she was mine, just like this house and Granny and everything else this other family seemed to be borrowing for the day. But then Heather looked up at me with a smile that dimpled her cheeks just like mine did, and I felt the anger melt away.

"We can share," I found myself saying. "Sisters share, right?"

Miss Margaret's sharp intake of breath made me look up. She was blinking fast, like Granny did when trying not to cry. "Yes," she said softly. "Sisters do share."

Granny interjected behind me, "Trisha, why don't you play with Heather in your room? Let Margaret and I catch up."

"Okay, Granny." I stretched out my hands toward Heather, and she willingly took mine. I looked toward Miss Margaret, and something in her widened stare made me say, "It's alright. I will take care of her," before I led her away to my bedroom.

Inside my room, Heather and I sat cross-legged on the floor with my dolls scattered around us. The afternoon light filtered through my window, casting long shadows across the faded rug. I could hear the murmur of adult voices from the gallery, their tones rising and falling like waves.

Footsteps in the hallway drew closer—first, the heavy, measured stride I recognized as my grandfather's, then another set matching his pace. More footsteps approached from the gallery's direction, and suddenly, my doorway was crowded with faces: my father, grandfather, Granny, and Miss Margaret, all watching Heather and me play as if they'd stumbled upon something precious and painful.

The silence stretched between us until Granny gently said it was time for them to leave. I stood, still holding my favorite doll, as they filed out, moved down the hall and through the drawing room, never pausing as they headed out the front door to the gallery.

From there, I watched as he got into his shiny red car. The same color as the hibiscus flower I'd picked for him, the same color I'd told him was my favorite. The car grew smaller and smaller until it disappeared around the bend, taking him away again.

* * *

"I hate red now," I announced suddenly, my voice sharp and clear in the heavy evening air.

Granny looked down at me, her gaze soft and understanding. "Is that so?"

"Yes." I yanked one red ribbon from my hair, realizing I lost one sometime during the day. I'd worn the two ribbons around my pom-pom hairstyle; had chosen them special for him. "Red is a lying color. It pretends to be pretty but it just goes away."

Granny didn't argue. She gathered me close, her familiar scent of bay leaf and coconut oil wrapping around me like a shield.

That same evening, I found Granny in the gallery, crying as an old record played in the living room. When I asked her what was wrong, she pulled me close and said, "Nothing, child. I'm just remembering when your father used to play music that made the whole neighborhood dance."

"Will the Cascadura bring him back?" I whispered.

She was quiet for a long moment, her hand stroking my hair. "Some people," she finally said, "carry Trinidad in their blood no matter what they eat. And some..." She sighed. "Some need more than fish to find their way home."

As she cleaned up later that night, I noticed she'd saved some of the leftover Cascadura. "For tomorrow," she said with a wink, "because you and me? We never leaving this island. It's in our bones."

She was right. Even then, I could feel the rhythm of Trinidad beating in my chest like a steel drum, steady and true. I might not have had my father, but I had Granny and this island. Sometimes, that was enough to make my heart feel full, even when it was busy learning how to hate the color red.

Chapter 10—Mary and Cecil

January 1978, Dry Season

How many times can a mother's love cross an ocean before it begins to falter? Every evening, I asked myself that question while watching Cecil on the veranda, his pipe smoke rising like prayers into the heavy air. It haunted me each time I sealed another letter to Joromi or watched Trisha run for the phone, hoping to hear her father's voice. The calendar on the wall marked another week until his next call—if he could manage it that month.

Still, my mind automatically crafted excuses for my son, my granddaughter's father. *International rates are steep; sometimes, even a father's love has to bow to empty pockets.*

I stepped onto the veranda to join my husband. "You were brooding again," I said softly to Cecil, trying for a playful tone that fell flat.

He looked up, his eyes narrowing as he pulled the pipe from his mouth. "I was just thinking about the boy. It had been two and a half years since he last gave us half a day. The calls helped, but a child needed more than a voice on the phone once a month."

My fingers pinched the edge of my latest unfinished letter to Joromi. I wrote to him faithfully every month, filling pages with Trisha's small triumphs—her grades, her growing love of reading, the way she had started helping me in the kitchen. I did everything I could so that he wouldn't forget—so that their distance did not grow beyond what could be reconciled. On the cool afternoon breeze, I heard her laughter mingling with the neighbor children's voices as they played in the street before bedtime. The sound twisted something in my heart.

I rested my hands on my lap over the paper. Taking a deep breath, I let my gaze wander to the garden. "Do you think it was my fault?" I asked.

Cecil's head turned sharply. "What kind of question was that, Mary?" he replied.

"It had been on my heart," I admitted, my voice barely above a whisper. "I had never told Joromi about... about how you and I met. How he came before we exchanged our vows." I turned to face Cecil. "I wondered if I should have told him. Maybe it would have helped him be brave enough to do things differently."

Cecil's brow furrowed as he leaned forward, placing

his pipe on the small table between us. "You had been holding that in all that time?"

I nodded, my fingers twisting together. "We had been older when we met. I had been so sure of myself but lost in so many ways—desperate to be a mother. I fell for you the moment I saw you at that party, Cecil. You were the most handsome man in the room—tall, skinny, and hairy, laughing as if you didn't have a care in the world. I remembered thinking, 'This man would be a great father.' How I knew that, I didn't know. But I didn't care about anything else."

Cecil chuckled. "I always said, you were a hunter and you trapped a lion that night."

We laughed together, the sound rich and full, before falling into a quiet lull.

After a moment, I said, "He didn't really talk to his daughter on those calls, Cecil. He let me do all the talking. And when he spoke to her, he asked the same tired questions strangers asked little kids. Then, after the calls, Trisha asked me, every time, when she would see him again. When she could visit America."

I expelled my breath loudly and looked down at my half-written letter. "I never knew what to tell her."

At that moment, I also chose not to mention that Cecil never talked to Joromi. I refused to consider how much Joromi was like his father.

Cecil reached for my hand. "When we had decided to raise her, he had planned to visit more. To have her come up for summers now that she was bigger." He tapped his pipe against the ashtray with his other hand, setting it down. "The money he sent helped, and yes, he called when he could afford it. But a child needed more than that—needed to see her father's face, feel his presence."

When I spoke again, my voice sounded softer, almost like I was talking to myself. "Did you think we should have told Joromi about our storms? That before we found our calm, we had been a wildfire in dry season and a hurricane in the wet?"

"Did you think that made it your fault that he had impregnated a woman and ran off with another?" Cecil's tone was calm, but there was an edge to it. "Mary, plenty of people's beginnings weren't what they imagined they should be. That didn't make them wrong. What made them wrong or right was how they responded."

"But Joromi hadn't known about us," I insisted. My voice trembled despite myself. "He hadn't seen the love we had fought for, the sacrifices we had made to build that life. All he was... was a man who wanted everything flawless like he thought his parents' life was... he wanted what he saw as perfection."

Cecil leaned back, exhaling heavily. "And did you think that's why he was running? Why he was leaving his child behind? He had needed to marry a woman like you to be a man like me?"

My shoulders slumped. "Maybe. Maybe if I had told him, he would have seen that life wasn't always about perfect choices. It was about owning the imperfect ones and trying to do better. Now I wondered if I had failed him."

I thought again about Trisha's face when the phone

rang and how she ran to answer it, hoping it was her father. The monthly calls meant so much to her; the disappointment when they didn't come was painful to watch.

"Maybe in your next letter," Cecil suggested, squeezing my hand, "you needed to be more direct. Tell him we appreciated the calls, but he had to find a way to visit. This wasn't supposed to be us raising his child alone while he built a new life over there."

"I'd write him that night," I said firmly. "Tell him we were grateful he called, that we knew it was expensive. But also tell him Trisha needed more. We had expected more when we took her in."

In the street, I heard Trisha's voice rising in another verse of her song. I made a mental note to include that moment in my letter—another small piece of our granddaughter's life to transmit across the ocean.

Cecil squeezed my hand. "We raised her, Mary, because she was ours. First blood or second blood, she was ours then. And if Joromi ever pulled himself together, he would see that. Until then, we stood in the gap. That's what family did."

My tears fell silently, steady as a summer rain. I leaned my head on Cecil's shoulder, feeling the strength in him and the promise of his partnership. Together, we watched the fireflies dance over the garden, tiny lights shimmering against the darkness.

"Maybe," I whispered, "one day, Joromi would see his love with Maggie and Heather could grow big enough to include his first blood. And maybe he'd be brave enough to come back home."

Cecil said nothing, but his hand stayed firm on mine, anchoring me as the night deepened.

Perhaps a mother's love didn't fade across oceans after all. It just changed shape and became something fiercer, more demanding. Something that insisted on building bridges even when the shores seemed too far apart.

I rose and called, "Trisssshaaah, time to come inside, gurl!"

Chapter 11—Trisha

May 1980, Dry Season

The years passed like pages in my favorite storybook series by Enid Blyton, each filled with fast-paced adventures, though I preferred to experience them from the quiet comfort of our gallery rather than living them myself. Unlike other children who'd be playing in the yard, I found my joy in books and learning. Granny always said I had a mind like a steel trap—once I caught hold of something, I wouldn't let it go until I understood it completely. The other children called me "teacher's pet" or "bookworm," but I didn't mind; I found more companionship in stories and studies than in their games.

Maybe that's why I did so well in school. When my Common Entrance results came, Granny cried happy tears, and Daddy, which is what I called my grandfather, brought home a special ice cream cake from Hi-Lo in the Croisée. "First class honors!" they told everyone who would listen. "She passed for her first choice—seven years!" Even my teacher said she wasn't surprised; I always had my hand up first. But deep inside, beneath all the celebration, beneath my grown-up composure that made adults forget I was just a child, I wondered if this news would make it into one of those letters that went to America, and if it did, would my father feel proud?

There was a box hidden behind Granny's good china, wrapped in one of her old sari material. I found it while looking for the fancy teacups she only used when the Pastor visited. Inside were dozens of letters—all from America, all from him. Some had money tucked inside; others just words that made Granny's eyes go soft and sad when she read them.

I wasn't supposed to find where Granny stored them after she read them. Wasn't supposed to see how the ink had run in places, like tears had fallen while someone read them. Wasn't supposed to know that my father wrote things like "I'll send more next month" and "Tell her I'm thinking of her"—never writing my name, like I was just an afterthought at the bottom of a grocery list.

The rain drummed against our galvanize roof that afternoon, making that tin-pan music that usually helps me sleep. But the nap I wanted wouldn't come. Instead, I lay on my bed, holding one of his letters, trying to understand why someone who thinks about you doesn't want to know you.

* * *

"Daddy?" I asked my grandfather that evening as we sat in the gallery, watching sheets of rain turn our garden into a swamp. "Why do you let me call you Daddy when you're not really my father?"

His hands, rough from years of working in industrial spaces, stilled on his newspaper. The rain seemed to get louder in the silence that followed.

"Who says I'm not really your father?" he finally asked, his voice gentle but firm. "A father is someone who loves you, who teaches you, who's there when you fall down and need picking up. Being a father isn't just about first blood."

But I had more questions, like raindrops that wouldn't stop falling. "Then why did he leave? Why didn't he want to be my father too?"

Daddy folded his newspaper carefully, taking his time like he always does when something's important. "Sometimes people run from things that scare them," he said slowly. "Even good things. Even love."

"Did I scare him?" My voice came out smaller than I meant it to.

"No, child." He pulled me close, and I could smell the bay rum cologne he always wore. "He scared himself. There's a difference."

Later that night, I heard Granny and Daddy talking in the kitchen. Their voices mixed with the sound of rain on the roof.

"She's asking questions," Daddy said.

"Of course she is. She's getting big now—ten years old. Can't keep feeding her fairy tales about her father coming back." Granny's voice had that edge it gets when she's trying not to cry.

"What do we tell her then?"

"The truth. Or as much of it as she can hold right now."

* * *

The next morning, Granny found me in the kitchen eating Crix—a round, lightly salted cracker with a satisfying crunch—topped with a thick slice of rich, creamy cheese, its sharp, tangy flavor lingering with each bite. I had been trying to make coffee just the way she liked it, but the pot felt too heavy in my small hands. Somewhere between wrestling with it and nearly spilling, I gave up and settled at the table instead.

Granny didn't say a word. She simply took over, moving through the kitchen with the ease of someone who's done it a thousand times. Once the coffee finished percolating, she sat down across from me, her eyes soft but knowing.

"Your mother," she began, stirring her coffee slowly, "loved to dance in the rain. Said it made her feel clean and new." She looked out the window at the water still falling. "Your father, he loved to make people dance. Had a gift for knowing just what song would make a sad heart happy again."

I pushed my untouched tea—which was really Milo—around in the mug, watching as the rich, chocolatey drink curled in a leisurely whirl. Into the cup, I said, "But they didn't stay together."

"No," she said softly. "They didn't. Sometimes love isn't enough to make people brave."

"You are brave, Granny. I love you."

Granny stilled for a moment, her hand resting lightly on the edge of the table as if the weight of my words had caught her off guard. Her eyes, dark and full of stories she rarely told, softened, and she gave a small, trembling laugh—the kind that comes when tears aren't far behind.

"Since you were born, girl, I gone soft," she said, dabbing at her eyes with the hem of her apron. "Crying at every little thing like somebody put too much pepper in my heart."

She shook her head, but there was no hiding the pride that flashed across her face. Her hand found mine, warm and worn across the table, her thumb tracing small, absent circles over my knuckles.

"You make it easy to be brave, Trisha," she whispered, the tenderness in her voice curled around each word. "Loving you is the simplest thing I ever do."

* * *

That night, I put the letters back behind the china, wrapped in Granny's old sari. Let him keep his words on paper.

I no longer needed to unfold them, searching for scraps of the love he couldn't show in person. Granny's steady hands and soft humming in the kitchen were louder than all his unspoken apologies. Daddy's laughter — deep and unrestrained — was the kind of comfort I could hold on to.

I realized then that love didn't have to come in grand gestures or carefully written words. It was in the quiet moments, the ordinary mornings of Milo and Crix, and how Granny's eyes lingered on me a little longer when she thought I couldn't feel her loving gaze.

I didn't need to wait for someone who had left long ago. I was already whole and home, going to Secondary school in a few months. I was big now.

Yet, life has a way of challenging bold declarations, and a few years later, my trial arrived with a force that I could scarcely have anticipated.

Chapter 12—Trisha

May 1987, Dry Season

Everything changed at breakfast that morning. A new letter sat propped against the sugar bowl, my name written in that familiar slanted script I'd come to know from the stack of hidden letters behind Granny's good china. My father wanted me to visit him in New York after my graduation.

"What you think about that?" Granny asked, her voice gentler than I expected as she stirred her coffee. She looked at me directly, her eyes holding a mix of concern and what might have been hope.

I tapped the envelope against my palm. "I don't know," I said, even though I felt a tentative excitement as I considered this possibility.

Granny set down her coffee cup with deliberate care. "University is coming up soon," she said, more to her cup than to me. "Your grandfather and I have been talking…and with things so tight lately…" She trailed off, then squared her shoulders. "Maybe this is God opening a door."

I watched her hands, steady as they rested on the table. These same hands had braided my hair through the years, cooked my meals, and rubbed my face roughly to dry my tears. They'd held me through seventeen years of life, never wavering, never leaving.

Unlike his. *What do his hands even look like*, I wondered. Shaking my head and returning to the moment, I said, "Shauntelle and them talking about going abroad for university." Trying to keep my voice neutral, I continued, "Canada, maybe. Or England." *Not America.*

"Shauntelle's mother has money to burn." Granny nodded, then added quietly, "Your father… he has means now. He could help with your schooling." She got up to water her African violets on the windowsill, plants that thrived in her care despite the punishing heat. "And you are smart like anything. You are top of your class in Biology, just like him."

Outside, a Kiskadee bird called from the Julie mango tree — once, twice, three times. The sound carried memories of countless afternoons spent in its shade, doing homework while Granny shelled pigeon peas, telling me stories about my mother and father.

"She was just your age," Granny said suddenly, her voice soft with memory, "when she met your father. Seventeen and full of dreams bigger than this island could hold." She turned to face me, something fierce in her expression. "But you different. You got your head screwed on right. And opportunities she never had."

The words settled between us, heavy with potential rather than judgment. I knew what she was saying. Maybe I could succeed where my mother couldn't, and perhaps I could bridge the gap between dreams and reality.

But do I have to leave Trinidad to do that? My mind ran to Rishi then, and I smiled without warning.

Sweet, steady Rishi was another dear friend. He played steelpan at the youth center on weekends and looked at me like I hung the moon. His hands constantly gesticulated in the air as if playing a phantom pan. And when we walked home together, he'd tell me about wanting to revolutionize pan music, make it something the whole world would recognize.

"We could do it right here, Trisha Sacks," he'd say, his eyes bright with conviction. He always called me by my first and last name. "Why everybody feel they have to leave to make something of themselves?"

But even Rishi's family was struggling. His father had been laid off from the sugar factory, and his sister had already dropped out of UWI because they couldn't afford the fees.

I did not realize a few moments of silence had passed, and Granny was watching me with an eagle's eye. I straightened and averted my eyes, looking out the window into the yard.

The dry season had cracked open the earth in

Granny's garden, deep fissures running through the soil like the lines on a map. Sometimes, I felt those same lines running through me—daughter of a woman who dreamed too shallow, of a man who ran too far—standing between Granny's wisdom and my father's wealth, wondering if I could draw strength from both.

"Maybe," I said finally, "seeing what's out there doesn't mean leaving everything behind."

Granny's smile was slight but reached her eyes. "Just remember, child," she said, returning to her plants, "your roots here strong. Strong enough to help you grow wherever you go." She paused, then added, "And if your father want to help with that growing... well, maybe that's his way of trying to make things right."

The Kiskadee called again, its voice clear and insistent in the dry season air. I folded the letter carefully, tucking it away with all the others—no longer just a collection of maybes and might-have-been, but perhaps a bridge to something new.

That evening, when Rishi came by with his latest pan composition, he greeted me as always. "Good Evening, Trisha Sacks."

Whenever he said my full name like that, I wondered if somewhere in the ether, my mother turned to us. *Not you, Trisha Sacks*, I would say, *Is me he talking to.*

In the twilight, I sat on the steps and listened to him play, the notes rising sweet and clear into the gathering dark. Granny brought out sorrel and coconut bake, and for a moment, everything felt perfectly aligned—the music, the cooling air, the taste of home on my tongue.

But later, alone in my room, I read my father's letter again. The words seemed different now, less like an escape route and more like a possible path forward. Standing on the edge of my choices at seventeen, I wondered if this was how my mother felt—caught between the familiarity of what she knew and the thrill of what she didn't.

The difference was I didn't have to choose between them. Maybe I could be like Granny's African violets—rooted here in Trinidad soil but strong enough to flower anywhere. And maybe my father's offer wasn't just about money for university—maybe it was about building bridges across oceans of silence, finding ways to make peace with the past while walking toward the future.

Later that week, during lunch break, my best friend Amy and I sat on the school steps, sharing a *doubles* wrapped in wax paper. The spicy chickpea filling made my eyes water, but I welcomed the burn—it gave me an excuse for the tears threatening to fall.

"Miss Shields say we should focus on our education first," Amy said, licking channa from her fingers. "Bachelor's, Master's, even PhD before we even think about settling down." She nudged me with her shoulder. "That's why you so lucky, girl. All them boys know better than to waste your time when you busy being the next Marie Curie."

I laughed, but it felt hollow. The truth was, I wondered if anyone saw me at all. The straight-laced girl with her nose always in a book, the one who got perfect marks in Biology but couldn't hold a boy's attention if her life depended on it. Well, except Rishi, but that would never be. He fawned but made no moves. Sometimes, I'd catch myself watching couples in the schoolyard, how they leaned into each other, shared secret smiles, passed notes in class. I yearned for that kind of connection, that spark that had made my mother throw caution to the wind for love.

But Granny's warnings echoed in my head: "You can't be spreading your legs for any and everybody." What remained unsaid hung heavy in the air—*like your mother*. The weight of Granny's unspoken fears pressed against my chest whenever a boy so much as looked my way.

"But what if..." I started, then lowered my voice, "What if love finds you before all that? Like it found my mother?"

Amy's face softened. "That was different times, girl. Different world." She crumpled the wax paper into a tight ball. "Besides, you think any boy round here good enough for you? You need somebody who could match your brain and your heart."

I thought about my father's letter, still sitting on my dresser at home. The invitation to New York felt both like an opportunity and a trap. *What would it be like, staying with a man who was essentially a stranger? A stepmother I'd only met once? A half-sister who probably resented my very existence?*

"Amy," I whispered, "What if I go up there and they don't like me? What if..." I swallowed hard, "What if *he* doesn't like me?"

"Then that's his loss," she said firmly. "But girl, you can't spend your whole life wondering 'what if.' Your mother took a chance on love and maybe it didn't work out how she planned, but at least she lived. She loved." Amy squeezed my hand. "And look what came out of it—you."

The rest of the dry season stretched ahead, full of possibility and promise but also full of questions I wasn't sure I was ready to answer. Soon, I would have to decide about university, New York, and the shape my dreams would take. I wondered whether I was brave enough to open my heart to love when it finally came, whether I could trust myself to choose better than my mother had, and whether I could face a father who had chosen another life, another family, over me.

But for the moment, I let the afternoon air carry the scent of curry and Amy's laughter, knowing that sometimes the heart can grow large enough to hold everything — roots and wings, past and future, fear and hope, and yes, even the courage to love.

Chapter 13—Trisha

February 1991, Dry Season

The frangipani tree in Granny's yard sprouted its flowers early that year. White petals with yellow centers scattered across the ground like stars fallen to earth, their sweet perfume mixing with the morning breeze. I'd been gathering them to make garlands—a habit from childhood—when a shiny, expensive car pulled up by the gate, its horn blaring through the peaceful morning air.

"Hello, good morning, Miss Sacks! I need you to come by the office today, okay?"

I looked up and saw the face of an immaculately made-up woman leaning out the car's back window, her face unusually serious. I was always shocked at how sweat never escaped through her pores. She was our neighbor and an attorney specializing in immigration matters.

My hands stilled, petals dropping from my fingers. After four years of paperwork, appeals, and endless trips to her office, I knew what this meant. Another dead end. Another form to file. Another reason why my father's bastard daughter couldn't get approval to study in America.

"Let me guess—they need more proof?" The words tasted bitter. "More evidence that the man who didn't give me his name, whose signature isn't on my birth certificate, is really my father?"

Her silence and sad smile were answer enough for me.

Granny called from the gallery, "Stop that talking nonsense, Trisha." She hollered to the car, "Good Morning, Miss Johnson. Thanks for everything, eh!"

Later that evening, as I sorted files at my clerk's desk in the Ministry of Justice, I thought about how life had its own way of drawing boundaries. Four years of working here had taught me more about legal systems than I ever wanted to know. Every day, I processed other people's documents and helped them navigate the bureaucracy that had become my personal maze.

"You too smart for this clerical work," Granny would say whenever I came home late, my eyes tired from reading the fine print. She'd push a plate of pelau toward me, adding, "Your father was bright in school, you know. Just like you."

Yes, I knew.

I was halfway through my bachelor's degree at UWI, paying my way with this government job. The irony wasn't lost on me—working in justice while feeling the weight of injustice. But there was freedom in it, too. Every paycheck was mine. Every grade I earned belonged to me alone.

Chapter 14—Trisha

March 1991, Dry Season

Then, a phone call triggered a cascade of events I never saw coming.

"Trisha?" An unfamiliar woman's voice, an American accent. "This is Miss Margaret...your father's wife."

I suddenly felt dizzy.

"He's sick, Trisha. The doctors say..." Her voice cracked. "It's prostate cancer. Advanced. He's asking for you."

I pressed my palm flat against the desk to steady myself. Through the office window, I could see the frangipani tree in the courtyard, its branches heavy with blossoms. Life and death, always dancing so close.

"I can't come," I said, the words scraping my throat. "The paperwork—"

"I know," she cut in. "He told me everything. About the birth certificate, the name…" She paused. "He's not proud of it, Trisha. Any of it. But can you speak with hi—"

"No!" I cut her off. "No, not right now."

When my father chose not to come to Trinidad for my high school graduation, I stopped speaking to him. I cut him off, cold. *What was there to say? Nothing.* He did not push to reconcile. I suppose he agreed. Even as we worked together on the immigration paperwork, I communicated through Miss Johnson. I told myself that when we see each other again, we could say everything that needs to be said.

Now, he wants to talk to me? What in the world would he want to say?

"Miss Margaret?"

"Yes?"

"Tell him tomorrow is my birthday and my favorite color is black."

"Oh, shucks, I—"

I hung up before she could utter a sorry excuse for forgetting.

That night, I sat with Granny on the gallery steps, watching the sunset paint the sky in shades of guilt and grace.

"You remember what I always tell you?" she asked, her hand warm on my knee. "About your mother?"

I nodded. *How could I forget?*

"That she loved big, with frenetic restlessness, and left beautiful."

"Yes."

Granny's voice was soft. "But I never tell you this part—your father, he loved her too. Too much, maybe. Scared him so bad he run away from it." She squeezed my knee. "Sometimes people do foolish things when love feel too big to hold."

Was she talking about me? I wondered but did not ask.

The next few weeks passed in a blur of hospital updates from Miss Margaret. Each call brought news of my father's declining health, each one making the distance between us feel both vast and meaningless. I found myself looking at old photographs more often, searching my face for traces of him, wondering if he was doing the same with memories of me.

The frangipani kept flowering, each new blossom a reminder that life moves in cycles—death and renewal, loss and growth. I gathered the fallen flowers each morning, arranging them in water-filled bowls around the house, their sweet scent a constant reality as I waited for news I didn't want to hear.

"He's asking for you again," Miss Margaret said in what would be her final plea. Her voice sounded tired. I supposed it was heavy because of the weight of keeping vigil. "He's trying to hold on, Trisha. Trying to find the words…"

I couldn't listen to her anymore, so I handed the

phone to Granny. In my young adult mind, some distances couldn't be crossed by words alone. Some bridges take more time to build than we're given. *I'm not ready to talk to him.* I knew this, even as I hoped fate would stretch to give us time.

That evening, as the setting sun painted the San Juan sky in shades of amber and rose, I stood in our yard while Granny watered her plants. Suddenly, tears welled in my eyes, and an anguished cry erupted. She dropped the hose and hurried over. Being shorter than I was, she wrapped her arms around my waist, pinning my arms at my sides, and I rested my chin on top of her head. After a moment, she loosened her embrace, stepped back, and gazed into my water-logged eyes.

"You know what I see when I look at you?" Granny asked, wiping my tears with her thumbs. "I see your mother's fire and your father's strength. Both of them, living in you. And child…" she smiled, "you wearing it better than either of them ever did."

A breeze stirred the branches above us, sending a shower of white petals swirling around us like blessings. Or maybe like promises—that love, in all its forms, keeps growing, keeps finding ways to heal what was broken.

I picked up a fallen blossom, touching its delicate petals. In its five-pointed perfection, I saw a map of my own heart: one point for the father I barely knew, one for the mother who loved without limits, one for the grandmother who never wavered, one for the girl I was, and one for the woman I was becoming.

Standing there, surrounded by falling flowers and fading light, I felt something shift in my soul. It was a certainty that although I carried their stories in my blood, my own story was still unfolding. Whatever came next— whatever words my father might find or fail to speak—I was ready to face it with my own truth.

The phone rang inside the house, its sharp trill cutting through the evening peace. Granny's hand found mine, squeezing tight, as we both somehow knew what news awaited us. Daddy came out in short order. "Mary, Trisha come and take this call."

Margaret's voice was thick with tears when she told us he was gone. But what followed surprised us both—he'd asked to be buried in Trinidad.

"He said it was where he was meant to rest in the end," Miss Margaret explained. "Where his roots were."

Granny made a sound between a laugh and a sob. Later that night, I found her in the kitchen, staring into her tea like it held answers.

"You know what funny?" she said, not looking up. "Your father eat Cascadura fish when he was young. They say anybody who eat it must return to end their days in Trinidad." She shook her head slowly.

The days that followed brought an unexpected outpouring of support. Amy took leave from work to help with arrangements. My UWI classmates formed a rotating schedule, making sure someone was always with me. Even my supervisor at the Ministry gave me all the time I needed.

Rishi came every evening with his guitar, playing soft melodies in the gallery while others gathered. Sometimes, he'd play old kaiso songs that made Granny smile through her tears. "Music heals," he'd say, "even when words fail."

The funeral was on a Thursday. The Cathedral of the Immaculate Conception was packed — faces I knew mixed with strangers who'd known my father in his youth. The morning light filtered through stained glass, painting rainbow patterns across the pews.

That's when I saw her — Miss Margaret — walking toward me with an envelope in her hands. Her eyes were red-rimmed.

"He wrote this," she said softly, holding out the envelope. A faded but still vibrant red ribbon was tied around it in a simple bow. "In those last weeks. Made me promise to deliver it myself." She hesitated, then added, "He wanted you to know… he tried to find the right words for twenty-one years. These were the ones he finally found."

The envelope felt heavy in my hands, weighted with decades of silence finally broken. I didn't open it there. Some words need their own space, their own time.

Heather stepped out from behind Miss Margaret. Even though we'd met only once before — when I was five and she was two — something about her felt instantly familiar. It could have been how her dark hair curled out from her head as if stretched to the world's four corners and every angle in between — just like mine when I let it be.

At first, neither of us said anything. Then, without warning, we moved at the same time, pulled by a force we couldn't name. We fell into each other's arms, hugging fiercely, as though a single embrace could bridge the distance of two decades.

I felt her trembling. Or maybe it was me. My cheek brushed against her shoulder and I caught the faint scent of lilies—probably from the flowers arranged around the cathedral. She whispered, her American accent soft but distinct, "Trisha… I'm so sorry."

I tightened my hold around her. "I'm sorry too," I managed, my voice quivering. "We…we should've had more time."

We pulled apart slowly. Heather dabbed at her eyes with a handkerchief edged in lace. She seemed uncertain, glancing at the casket and then at me. "I wish…" she started, but the sentence trailed off.

I looked at the letter in my hands. The red ribbon had loosened slightly, the edges of the envelope already growing warm from my grip. "Should we—do you think—" I began, unsure if I wanted to read my father's final words in such a public space.

Heather shook her head gently, as if reading my thoughts. "He said it was for you. And you alone." Her voice was hushed, apologetic. "We can… talk. After."

I swallowed hard and nodded. Looking at Miss Margaret, who was crying silently and looking at us, I said, "Thank you for bringing it."

Across the aisle, Auntie June—our father's cousin— motioned for us to join the small group gathering near the side door. It was almost time for the final blessings. The priest was preparing to lead the pallbearers out.

Heather and I began to walk together, side by side, the hush of the cathedral strangely comforting. Neither of us spoke as we made our way down the aisle. The thick scent of incense hung in the air, mixing with the grief that pulsed through the pews.

We paused near the carved wooden doors as the pallbearers lifted the casket. I felt emotion wring my chest, and I burst into tears again. This was the father I'd barely known, the father Heather had known in a different way — perhaps better, perhaps not. Heather looked at me with tears in her eyes, and I fell into her arms again.

She whispered into my ear, "He tried to do better. I know he had regrets." She exhaled, the sound shaky. "But it's not my place to speak for him."

I bit my lip, tasting salt. "I know," I whispered back, proud of her for being so mature. I immediately felt love for her.

Auntie June was ushering the last of the mourners outside. The midday light streaming through the cathedral doors felt too bright after the dim interior. Music, quiet yet resonant, drifted toward us, marking the final procession.

We turned to follow, stepping into the sunlight. The casket moved ahead, carried by men in dark suits. White petals were tossed onto the path before them.

I watched as one of the pallbearers — my grandfather — struggled beneath the weight of the casket. His shoulders, always so straight and proud, trembled with each step. For the first time in my life, I saw him cry, tears sliding silently down his weathered face as he helped carry his only son's body. Behind me, I heard a soft sob and turned to see Miss Margaret holding my Granny, their arms wrapped around each other like old friends. The sight pierced my heart—my grandparents, who had given up their dreams of St. Croix to raise me, now faced the cruelest task any parent could face: burying their only child.

Outside, the streets of Port of Spain bustled with energy that was in stark contrast to our woeful mourning. Cars honked distantly, and the massive palm trees lining the avenue rustled with a breeze. The cathedral bells began to toll, calling passersby to notice that a life had ended.

The origin of my life…had…ended.

Chapter 15—Joromi

<hr>

Song of a Father's Soul

My Dearest Trisha,

I pray this letter finds its way to you, even as I know I may not be here when you read it. There is so much I need to say—things I should have said long ago but didn't know how. This cancer in me causes water to stop and start to flow from me in the most painful ways. The pain, somehow, has unlocked words festering in my heart since you were born twenty-one years ago.

So, I write them now, hoping the words rushing out from my heart carry the truth my actions often failed to show. I feel compelled to confess the truth before I step into my next life.

You were conceived in love, Trisha. Your mother and I burned bright—perhaps too bright to last, but bright enough to light the world for a time. You are the evidence of love. In you, light lived and bloomed despite my actions and inaction. You are the living proof of all that was beautiful between us.

I love you.

I'm shaking my head right now, knowing you must doubt this.

But, Trisha, I have always loved you.

I felt for a long while I couldn't reveal this love. I let shame, pride, fear, and, in retrospect, stupid reasons get in the way. That was a mistake among many, and I am deeply sorry for all of them. I am sorry for not being the father you deserved, for not standing tall when you needed me most. Most of all, I am sorry I abandoned you.

But as I sit here, facing the end of my time on this plain, there is one thing I must tell you — a learning from what I did and did not do. My only message: follow your passion, Trisha. Whatever sets your soul on fire, whatever makes you feel alive — chase it with everything you have. Life is too short to live by someone else's rules. Don't stifle your instincts and intuition or bury your dreams under the weight of expectation.

Know this too — my love was never divided between you and Heather. A father's heart expands; it doesn't split. I dream that one day, you two might find each other, might build the bridge I did not construct in my lifetime.

No matter what, Trisha, be bold. Be fearless. And always, always let your heart guide you.

With all the love I never showed,

Your Father,

Joromi Enoch

Chapter 16—Rishi

June 1991, Dry Season

I found her in her usual spot behind the music building, where the poui trees blanketed the ground with their pink petals. My fingers absently brushed against the guitar pick in my pocket—a nervous habit I'd developed since realizing my feelings for her had grown beyond friendship.

The late afternoon sun caught her profile as she read what I knew must be her father's letter again. My heart ached watching her trace the words with her finger, as if trying to pull meaning from more than just the ink. I adjusted my wire-rimmed glasses, suddenly aware of how my freshly pressed shirt clung to my shoulders in the humid air. At twenty-two, I was still lanky despite my height, my skin the warm brown of over-steeped tea—a shade lighter than my father's but darker than my late mother's had been.

"Thought I'd find you here," I said, settling beside her on the concrete step. The distance between us felt both too much and not enough. Trisha looked up, and I found myself struck again by her beauty—how her dark eyes caught the light, how her curls framed her face. I'd watched her grow from the shy girl in Trinidad History class into this strong, brilliant woman, and somewhere along the way, my heart had decided on its own path.

"Want to talk about it?" I asked, reaching for the letter when she offered it. My father's words echoed in my head: "Beta, some lines aren't meant to be crossed." He never said it directly, but I knew he meant more than just the cultural divide between our Hindu family and Trisha's Christian one—the weight of generations of expectations pressed against my shoulders.

But as I read her father's words, I thought about my own loss—my mother, taken too soon by cancer when I was twelve. Before I could stop myself, I told Trisha about the red sari, how my mother would wear it every Divali, and the photographs that still lined our walls. I described how she'd stack her bangles up her arms until they sang with every movement, remembering how their music would mix with the smell of curry and cardamom in our kitchen.

In all our years of friendship, this was the first time I had spoken about my mother's death. "My pan music…" I declared, my voice taking on that passionate tone it always did when I talked about the instrument born in Trinidad, "I love playing this old calypso song my mother used to love—"Red, Red, Red." I started playing it one day, and instead of hurting, it felt like…like she was there with me, you know? Like the color wasn't just about loss anymore, but about keeping her spirit alive."

As I continued to speak, I watched Trisha's face soften, saw her fingers touch the red ribbon at her wrist. The urge to reach out and trace that same path with my fingers was almost overwhelming. Instead, I talked about pan music, about finding healing in the rhythms that belonged to all of us on this island, regardless of where our ancestors came from.

Yuh babbling boy! I paused, cutting myself off with silence.

"I never knew her," she said. Looking up at me, she clarified, "My mother."

I knew there was more, so I stayed quiet and waited for it.

"But Granny says she loved red too. She wore red dresses. When she wasn't wearing red dresses, she wore a red scarf to hold her massive afro. When she wasn't wearing the dress or the scarf, Granny said she had a pair of brown leather slip-on sandals with a blood-red adjustable buckle on her feet."

I saw tears pricking at the corners of her eyes.

"Maybe that's why my father couldn't look at me properly. I must have reminded him too much of her."

After thinking about what she said for a moment, I responded, "Or maybe he saw too much of himself in you. That letter—it's not just about regret, Trisha. It's about fear. It sounds like he was admitting he was afraid." I turned to face her fully. "But you're not afraid, are you? Not anymore."

"No."

Her tone was resolute, as if she was realizing what she said was true. We were quiet again. I looked around the grounds surrounding around us, reveling in our togetherness. It was the first time we had a chance to connect since the week of funeral preparation at her house.

"Rishi?"

I looked at her when her sweet voice said my name.

"I'm not moving to America. I don't need to chase his approval or try to fix what he broke." She touched the red ribbon tied around her wrist. "You know," she started with a choked tone, "I realized this ribbon was the same one Granny had used to tie my hair the day I first met my father. He'd wrapped it around the envelope Miss Margaret gave me at the funeral, faded but perfectly pressed after all these years. He'd kept it, Rishi…all this time. He carried it with him to America, held onto it through decades of silence."

I did not know what to say about this. I raised my eyebrows, shaking my head from side to side, and whistled a loud exclamation.

After a few long seconds of silence, I said, "My mother loved red just like yours." I hesitated, choosing my next words carefully. "Maybe that's why we understand each other so well, Trisha. We both know what it's like to bear the weight of someone who isn't with us as if they never really left."

When she smiled at me, I felt something shift

between us. The afternoon light caught the deep brown of her skin, making it glow like burnished copper. I wondered what my father would say if he could see her as I did—not as someone different but as the woman who made my world make sense.

"And the forgiveness?" I asked gently, knowing how she struggled with her father's not being around and now his death cementing the fact that he will never be a part of her life. "How's that coming?"

After a thoughtful moment, she said, "It's like learning a new pan arrangement, you start slow, hit some wrong notes, but eventually..." She smiled at me again. "Eventually, you find the rhythm that was there all along."

Dis girl using pan music as a metaphor? Lawd Fadda! That was Trisha—always finding ways to connect our worlds, to make space for both our stories in the same song. She also said she was going to stay in Trinidad; this caused something inside me to leap with hope.

My fingers moved of their own accord, barely brushing her ribbon-wrapped wrist. "Your mother chose red," I said softly, thinking of my own mother's boldness in keeping her traditions alive in a changing world. "Your father ran from it. But you, Trisha—you're choosing to understand it, to wear it your own way."

Pink petals floated down around us like blessings, and I imagined what my mother would say if she were here. She'd always told me that love was love, no matter what shape it took. "Follow your heart, beta," she used to say, bangles chiming with every gesture. "The rest will follow."

But the evening was waning, and I had steelpan

practice. "Good Evening, Trisha Sacks," I said, standing reluctantly. My heart thundered as I dusted off my pants, wondering if she could hear it.

"Play 'Red, Red, Red' for me sometime."

A smile tugged at my lips. "You got it, Trisha Sacks," I said, then forced myself to walk away before I did something foolish like kiss her under the falling poui blossoms.

As I rounded the corner of the music building, my hands already itching for the comfort of playing my steelpan, I thought about what my father would say. But for the first time, I realized that maybe some traditions were meant to be challenged, and some loves were worth being brave for.

The sun was setting as I headed to practice, painting the sky in shades of red and gold, and I found myself humming our song—the one I hadn't played for her yet but would. Soon.

Chapter 17—Trisha

July 1991, Rainy Season

"Read it again, child." My grandmother's voice was soft but insistent as she settled into her favorite chair in the gallery. The evening breeze stirred the hem of her house dress, carrying the sweet scent of the green lemon tree my grandfather planted when my father was born.

I unfolded the letter, now creased along familiar lines from the many times I'd opened and closed it since the funeral three months ago. The paper felt delicate between my fingers, as if my father's words might dissolve if I handled them too roughly.

"'My Dearest Trisha,'" I began, the words trembling on my lips despite my efforts to modulate my tone. My grandfather paused his slow rocking in the chair beside us, his work-worn hands folding in his lap.

As I read, I blinked up periodically at their faces. My grandmother's eyes glistened, but her chin remained high, proud even in her grief. My grandfather's expression was complicated, hard to read, carved deep with years of holding back words he maybe wished he'd said sooner.

"'You were conceived in love, Trisha,'" I continued, and my grandmother nodded, a small smile playing on her lips.

"That part is true," she said, patting my hand. "Your mother…she lit up every room she walked into. And your father? Lord, I never seen him so alive as when he was with her. I was always surprised that they did not end up together."

My grandfather cleared his throat. "I was wrong about her," he said, his voice rough with emotion. "Wrong about a lot of things." He looked at me directly then, something he rarely did. "I pushed your father to be what I thought a man should be. Steady job, meek wife, everything planned out neat and clean. Used to tell him he was wasting his smarts—boy had such a gift for the sciences, could've been something in the medical field. But life…" He shook his head. "Life don't always fit in the boxes we try to put it in."

"'Follow your passion,'" I read from the letter, and my grandmother made a sound between a laugh and a sob.

"Just like his mother's boy," she said, reaching for my grandfather's hand. "Always knew what was right, even when he was doing wrong. Had to learn it the hard way, but he learned it."

"We all did," my grandfather added quietly. He squeezed my grandmother's hand, then looked at me again. "Your grandmother here, she knew better than both of us men. Knew that love don't care about the best laid plans. She took care of your mother when everyone else turned away. Loved you like her own when…" His voice cracked slightly. "When we should have all been there."

It was my grandmother's turn to squeeze his hand. "Don't you go blaming yourself for any of it now," she said to him, her voice firm but gentle. "We all did what we thought was right at the time. Even if we was wrong." She turned to me, her eyes glistened with unshed tears. "But your father, he learned the biggest lesson of all, even if it took him too long to say it. Love ain't about being proper or right. It's about being true and present."

I folded the letter carefully and tucked it back into my purse. The sun was setting now, painting the sky in shades of orange and pink.

"I'm going to a party tonight," I said, standing up. "A pool party in Westmoorings."

My grandmother's eyes sparkled knowingly. "Is your mother's favorite color you wearing under that white dress, ent?"

I smoothed down my dress, feeling the red bikini beneath it. "How did you know?"

She smiled a warm smile that crinkled the corners of her eyes. "Because you your mother daughter. And your father daughter too. Got both their fire in you."

My grandfather stood, slower now with age but still

tall and strong. "Your father wrote true in that letter, you know. About following your heart." He looked at my grandmother, and something passed between them, decades of love and understanding distilled into a single glance. "We learn too late sometimes that the heart knows better than the head."

I hugged them both, breathing in the gentle aroma of coconut oil and bay leaf that clung to my grandmother, feeling my grandfather's strong arms around me, no longer stiff, his squeeze unusually tender.

"Go on," my grandmother said, gently pushing me. "Go find what makes your soul catch fire."

As I walked to my car, I heard my grandfather's voice, soft but clear in the evening air. "She got her mother's walk, but Lord, that smile pure him."

I touched the letter in my purse one last time before driving off, feeling its power like a talisman. Since I received it at his funeral, it was always with me. My father had hidden from love, run from passion, and tried to live life in safe, careful boxes. His final gift to me was the wisdom to choose differently, and I held on tight to this sentiment.

* * *

I stepped out of the car at Westmoorings, adjusting the strap of my bag. I wasn't sure what to expect from this pool party, but my skin tingled as if it knew something I didn't.

The music hit me before anything else, rolling through the open gates of the house like a wave. Soca mixed with dancehall, a rhythm that made your heart skip before it caught up. The bass thumped in time with my pulse as I stepped inside, scanning the scene: a sea of bikinis and linen shirts, the scene thick with laughter, rum, and the unmistakable scent of barbecue.

And then I saw him.

The DJ.

Positioned at the center of the deck, he commanded the space with an energy that belonged to this new decade. His hands hovered over the turntables, coaxing the beat into something that felt alive, breathing. His body moved with the rhythm, a symphony of muscle and intent, as though the music were simply a part of him.

But it was his face that caught me.

A sharp jawline softened by dimples that threatened to show with every near-smile. His skin gleamed under the glow of string lights strung across the yard, its honey-gold hue so warm it felt like it had been kissed by the very sun we'd all been trying to escape.

He looked up. Our eyes met, and everything else—the evening's voices and music—fell away.

There was nothing coy about his gaze. It wasn't the lightening look of someone trying to be subtle nor the rehearsed charm of someone used to getting what they wanted. No, his stare was deliberate, unhurried, as if he were deciding whether I was worth the next few moments of his life.

I swallowed hard, suddenly hyper-aware of the sheen of sweat on my neck, the way my dress clung to me in all the wrong places. I'd thrown on the flowy white number, thinking it would help me disappear into the background. It was a mistake because my red bikini underneath lit me up like a neon sign, all that vibrant color bleeding through the thin fabric, impossible to ignore. His eyes trailed down my figure, a slow, unapologetic sweep that left warmth rising in my cheeks.

His mouth curved slightly as if he'd noticed my discomfort and found it amusing. Or endearing. I couldn't tell which.

At that moment, the words from my father's letter floated across my mind's eye. *Follow your passion, Trisha. Whatever sets your soul on fire, whatever makes you feel alive — chase it with everything you have.*

I was astonished that after years of erasing Joromi Enoch from my memories, blocking out every fiction of his existence, a single letter — delivered by my stepmother in a most perfunctory manner at his funeral — could so completely resurrect him. Now, impossibly, his voice possesses my thoughts, and his perspective haunts my understanding of what is happening in my life.

So, this time, unlike my father with my mother, I wouldn't run from what I felt. I wouldn't let fear, propriety, or anyone else's expectations hold me back.

My feet moved before my brain caught up. One step, then another, the sound of gravel crunching beneath my sandals barely audible over the pounding in my chest. I didn't have a plan. *What would I even say?*

Perhaps, *Hi, I'm seeing you in a new light. I saw you from across the way and thought you should know you're messing with my equilibrium. Ridiculous!*

But there was no stopping me now.

The music shifted, and a familiar soca classic bled into the mix — the kind that made you feel like Carnival was a state of mind rather than a season. It filled the space between us, and my heartbeat synced with the beat as I wove through the crowd.

He kept watching me as I moved toward him. How could he be playing music and watching me like this? I could feel his gaze. His head tilted slightly, curiosity sparking in his eyes as though he hadn't expected me to cross the invisible line between us.

I reached the edge of the deck, the makeshift barrier separating him from the rest of us. He leaned forward slightly, his hand resting on the mixer, the other reaching for his headphones.

And then I smiled.

I really smiled this time. Not big, but not shy.

He slowly put down the headphones and stepped…to…me.

"What you doing here, Trisha Sacks?"

"Rishi Mohammed, you invited me, didn't you?"

An unexpected cool breeze swept over me then.

Carrying healing.

Like it was carrying a father home.

And carrying me toward my future, and I was ready to embrace whatever fire might come.

Part Three

Mother & Spirit Songs

Chapter 18—Mother & Amokye

First Verse

The river runs both ways here, like memory itself. Forward and backward, past and future tangled in its current. I watch my own reflection ripple and change—sometimes I'm the girl who danced into Joromi's fête that night, sometimes I'm heavy with child, and sometimes I'm as I was in my final moments when the pain and joy of bringing Trisha into the world consumed everything else.

Amokye sits beside me at the river's edge, her fishing line dancing in the water. They say she's been here since the beginning, fishing souls from the river, deciding which ones can cross to Asamando. Her eyes hold centuries of stories, and when she speaks, her voice carries the weight of all the souls she's guided.

"Trisha Sacks, you watch them too much," she says, not looking at me. "The living. It's not good for your spirit."

"They're still part of me. Plus, that boy, Rishi, just call my name," I answer, seeing Trisha in the tides—my daughter, grown now, wearing my favorite color, like a battle flag. "My death shaped them all."

Amokye's fishing line shivers. "Tell me," she says, "about the shaping."

The water shows me Joromi first, how my death cracked something in him that never quite healed. I see him in New York, trying to build a life with rules and order, but my ghost haunts his careful plans. "I didn't mean to break him," I whisper. "I cherished his untamed spirit and his music, but I became the reason he feared them both."

"And the child?" Amokye's voice is gentle now.

"Trisha?" Her name feels like sunlight on my tongue. "She got my fire but her grandmother's wisdom. Better combination, really." I laugh, but there's an unease in it. "Mary raised her right—taught her that love doesn't have to burn everything down to be real."

"You were young," Amokye says, drawing her line in. There is no fish today. No new souls are ready to cross.

"Young and too much." I trace patterns in the water. "That's what everyone said. Too loud, too boisterous, too hungry for life. But they didn't understand—I wasn't too much; I was exactly who I was meant to be. I just..." I pause, watching the memories swirl. "I just ran out of time to prove it."

The river shifts, showing me Mary—steady, strong Mary—taking my baby as her own. Teaching her to cook, to pray, to love carefully but completely. "She gave Trisha roots," I say. "While I gave her wings."

Amokye nods. "Both are needed for flying. One holding a place to rest and the other a way to soar."

I watch the living world through the river's lens—Trisha at the pool party, facing her attraction with courage instead of fear. Joromi, in his final days, finally finding words for all his unspoken loves. Mary and Cecil, who chose to stay when staying was the harder path.

"You know what's funny?" I tell Amokye. "They all think my story was a tragedy. Poor irresponsible girl, died too young, cautionary tale. But they're wrong." I stand up, feeling the rhythm of both worlds—the living and the dead—pulsing through me. "My love started a chain reaction. Trisha exists because I dared to love the fullness of life. She's strong because I died and Mary stepped up. She's brave because my death taught her that life is too precious for fear."

Amokye finally turns to look at me, her ancient eyes piercing and otherworldly. "And you? What did life and death teach you?"

I smile, feeling the truth of it all the way through my spirit. "That love doesn't end. It transforms. Every time Trisha chooses joy, every time she trusts her heart—that's me, living on. Every time Mary shares our story, every time Joromi's letter reaches across the divide—I'm there. Not as a warning, but as a promise."

"A promise of what?"

The river sings beneath us, carrying the sounds of both worlds—steelpan and spirits, heartbeats and history. "That being fully yourself is never a mistake. That love, in all its forms, is worth the risk. And that sometimes the most audacious choice is the truest one."

Amokye's laugh is like wind through bamboo. "Now you're ready," she says, standing. "Ready to stop watching and start flying."

I take her hand, feeling the pull of Asamando beyond the river. But before I go, I look one last time at the living world rippling below. My daughter stands at the edge of new love, wearing my red like a blessing. Joromi's words guide her forward instead of holding her back. And Mary watches it all, strong enough to let love grow in its fantastic way.

"Yes," I say, turning toward whatever comes next. "I think I am ready to fly with our spirits."

Chapter 19—Mother & Joromi

Second Verse

When Joromi crossed over, I felt it like music changing tempo. The river parted, and there he was—not the scared boy who ran from love, not the proper man he tried to become, but something in between. His spirit carried echoes of both our youth and his age, like a record playing two songs at once.

"Trisha?" His voice held all the questions we never got to ask each other.

"You remembered my name this time," I teased, the way I used to when we were young. "Not just 'that girl' anymore?"

He laughed—that deep, rich sound I'd almost forgotten—but there were tears in it. "I'm sorry," he said. "For everything. For not being brave enough. For-"

"Shh." I placed my hand over his heart, feeling the smoke of the rhythm that first drew me to him. "You found your courage in the end. That letter to our daughter? Perfection, sire!"

Amokye watched us from her perch by the river, her fishing line still. "Time moves differently here," she reminded us. "Show him."

I took Joromi's hands, and suddenly we were dancing again—like that first night at the fête, before fear and expectations got in the way. The river's surface gurgled with images: our daughter in her white dress with my red underneath, Mary's steady love shaping her into someone stronger than either of us, and all the moments we missed but somehow helped create.

"Look what we made," I whispered. "Not just Trisha, but this whole beautiful mess of love and growth and learning. You running away taught her to stand still. Me burning bright taught her how to tend her own flame."

"And my mother, Mary?" Joromi's voice was soft. "She did what we couldn't."

"She did what she was meant to do. Just like we did what we were meant to do. Even the painful parts had their purpose."

The music—real music, not just memory—rose around us. Steelpan and soul, calypso and jazz, and a talking drum carrying the rhythms underscoring our brief time together. Amokye's voice carried over it all. "Now you understand. Love doesn't need fixing. It needs freedom to become what it must."

Joromi held me closer, both of us swaying to the spirit songs. "I never stopped loving you," he admitted. "I just didn't know how to love that big."

"I know." I smiled up at him. "But our Trisha? She knows. Watch."

The river showed us one last glimpse: our daughter stepping toward her own love story, carrying both our lessons in her heart. She moved like me but thought like him—bold and wise, careful and free.

"She's better than both of us," Joromi said proudly.

"She's exactly who she's supposed to be." I stepped back, letting the dance end naturally this time. "Just like we were exactly who we were supposed to be—young, foolish, scared, brave, and everything in between."

Amokye's line finally pulled taut. "Time to cross," she called. "Both of you."

Joromi took my hand, and together, we faced the far shore of Asamando. "One last thing," I said, turning to him. "Thank you for naming her after me. Even if you never said it out loud, you kept me alive in her name."

"Trisha," he said, my name a blessing on his lips. "Let's go home."

* * *

Red, Red, Red (A Trinidad Calypso)

Verse:

Red like hibiscus in de morning light
Red like sunset when de day turns night
Red like memory dat burns so bright
Red like love dat holds you tight

Chorus:

Red, Red, Red
Flowing through my island head
Red, Red, Red
Like de stories mama said

Bridge:

Some people see red and tink of pain
But I see red like sweet sugar cane
Like flamboyant trees after de rain
Like old love coming home again

The traditional calypso rhythm, with steel drum accompaniment, followed the characteristic call-and-response pattern of Trinidad calypso music. It became Trisha and Joromi's soundtrack as they chip, chip, chip into their next lives.

Chapter 20—Trisha's Birthright

Chorus

I am Amokye, keeper of the river between worlds, fisher of souls. Since time began, I have watched the patterns of love and loss surge across generations. Here at my river's edge, all stories become one story. All waters flow into the same truth.

The mother blazed through life like summer lightning, her laughter still echoing in the spaces between worlds. She wore red like a second skin and danced as if the music would never end. The father built walls of propriety brick by brick until wisdom finally cracked their foundation. Between these extremes, their daughter found her rhythm.

I watch her now, this child of fire and stone. When she

steps toward the DJ, she moves with a grace born from both tempest and tide. Her red bikini glows beneath white cotton-like truth beneath pretense. She carries their song in her bones — all its sweet notes and bitter chords.

The young often ask me what their parents left behind. Some find freedom in the answer, and some find chains.

But this one — this Trisha — found a door. Through my ancient eyes, I see her standing at its threshold, where frangipani and poui blossoms fall, and music never dies. The DJ watches her with eyes that echo old stories, but this time, the melody writes itself differently.

My river flows on, as it has since the first ancestor drew breath. In Trinidad, their daughter lives between all the lessons, creating something new — note by note, beat by beat, love by love.

That is what they left behind: not an ending, but a beginning.

- Amokye, Keeper of the River Between Worlds

The End

A Note from The Author

Thank You for Reading!
→ PLEASE LEAVE A REVIEW

Beloved Reader,

Your support means the world to me.

Your feedback helps other readers find their next favorite read and inspires me to keep writing stories that resonate with you.

May we walk in unity, love, and wisdom.

Aşẹ and love,

Scarlet Ibis James

@scarlet.ibis.james

www.scarletibisjames.com

Glossary: Soul Clef

Words That Cross Waters & Worlds

Akan – An ethnolinguistic group of people who speak languages in the Kwa branch of the Niger-Congo language family. They live in Ghana, the Ivory Coast, and parts of Togo.

Amokye – In Akan mythology, the gatekeeper of the spirit world who sits by the river of death. She fishes for souls and decides which ones can cross to the afterlife.

Asamando – In Akan mythology, the realm of the ancestors and spirits; the afterlife.

Auntie – A respectful term used in Trinidad for any older woman, whether related by blood or not. More than just a title, it acknowledges the woman's role as an elder in the community and her right to offer guidance or correction to younger people. The term carries both affection and authority.

Bacchanal – More than just drama or scandal; in Trinidad culture, bacchanal describes the delicious chaos of public spectacle, especially when it involves romantic entanglements, family disputes, or community gossip. The term captures both the entertainment value and the social commentary aspects of public drama. Often used in phrases like "That is pure bacchanal!" to express both disapproval and secret enjoyment of the unfolding theatrical experience.

Calabash – A gourd that, when dried and hollowed, serves as a traditional vessel in Caribbean culture. Often used ceremonially and symbolically, representing wisdom and community.

Callaloo – A popular Caribbean dish made with leafy vegetables, particularly dasheen leaves, okra, and coconut milk.

Cascadura – A freshwater fish native to Trinidad; local legend says that anyone who eats it must return to Trinidad to end their days.

Chadon beni – An herb commonly used in Caribbean cooking, similar to cilantro but with a stronger flavor (also known as cilantro).

Chip – A distinctive way of moving to the music during Trinidad Carnival. It's a relaxed, rhythmic shuffle or short-step dance that masqueraders adopt while parading, keeping the feet close to the ground and swaying in time with the soca or calypso beats.

Commesse – Drama, confusion, or scandal; usually involving multiple people and resulting in public chaos. Unlike bacchanal, which can be celebratory, commesse almost always has a negative connotation. Often used in phrases like "doh start commesse" (don't start trouble) or "pure commesse in dat house" (nothing but drama in that house). Derived from the French word "commencer" (to begin/start).

Crix – A popular brand of crackers in Trinidad & Tobago, often eaten with cheese or butter.

Croisée – A bustling commercial hub and crossroads in San Juan, Trinidad, known for its vibrant street vendors, small shops, and lively atmosphere. The Croisée serves as a central meeting point for locals, offering a mix of goods, from fresh produce to household items, alongside rich cultural exchanges. Its name, derived from the French word for "crossroads," reflects its historical and contemporary importance as a central junction in the community.

Doubles – Popular Trinidadian street food made of two flat fried breads (bara) filled with curried chickpeas (channa).

Doux-doux – A term of endearment meaning "sweetie" or "darling."

drawing room – A formal sitting room or parlor in a Caribbean home, traditionally used for receiving and entertaining guests. Often furnished with the family's best furniture and decorative items, it was considered a more formal space than the gallery (veranda). It was typically kept closed off except for special occasions or important visitors.

Dry season – Trinidad and Tobago has two distinct seasons: a dry season from January to May and a rainy season from June to December.

Eh eh – An exclamation expressing surprise, disbelief, or emphasis; can also be used as a questioning "really?" or "is that so?"

Ent – A versatile word meaning "isn't it?" or "right?"; used at the end of sentences to seek agreement or emphasize a point.

Fadda – A Trinidadian pronunciation of "Father," often used in conjunction with "Lawd" (as in "Lawd Fadda!") to amplify an emotional response, such as astonishment, exasperation, or even comedic exaggeration.

Fête – A party or celebration (from the French "fête").

frangipani – A tropical flowering tree (also known as plumeria) common in Trinidad, known for its fragrant white and yellow blooms that appear during the dry season (February-May) and are incredibly aromatic in the evening.

Gallery – A veranda or porch, typically at the front of a Caribbean house.

Hi-Lo – A major supermarket chain in Trinidad & Tobago.

Joromi – A name of Yoruba origin. It was uncommon in the 1940s Trinidad and Tobago when the novella's character was born, yet the author chose it nonetheless.

Julie mango – A variety of mango popular in Trinidad, known for its small size and sweet taste.

Kaiso – Another word for calypso music; traditional Trinidad and Tobago folk music.

Kiskadee – A tropical bird common in Trinidad, known for its distinctive call.

Lawd – A colloquial Trinidadian pronunciation of "Lord," often used as an exclamation to express surprise, frustration, or disbelief. It's commonly part of everyday speech and carries a tone of heightened emotion.

Lime/liming – To hang out, socialize, or spend leisure time with friends.

Macocious – Nosy, meddlesome, or overly interested in others' business.

Mou mou/Mumu – A loose, comfortable dress commonly worn at home.

Oui – A word used at the end of sentences in Trinidad dialect, borrowed from French Creole, meaning "yes" or used for emphasis; often combined with "nah" as in "oui nah" to add friendly insistence or emphasis to a statement.

Pelau – A one-pot dish made with rice, pigeon peas, and meat, seasoned with Caribbean spices.

Pickney – Child (considered informal/dialect); offspring.

Pigeon peas – A type of legume commonly used in Caribbean cooking.

Poui – A cherished Trinidad tree known for its spectacular flowering season, when it sheds all its leaves and bursts into masses of pink or yellow blossoms. The pink poui (Tabebuia rosea) and yellow poui mark the change of seasons.

Rainy season – Trinidad and Tobago has two distinct seasons: a rainy season from June to December and a dry season from January to May.

Sorrel – A bright red beverage made from sorrel flowers (hibiscus), popular during Christmas.

Steups – A sound made by sucking air through the teeth to express annoyance or disapproval.

UWI – The University of the West Indies.

WASA – Water and Sewerage Authority of Trinidad and Tobago

Westmoorings – An upscale residential area in western Port of Spain, Trinidad, known for its waterfront properties and affluent community.

Wecquaesgeek – A Native American tribe of the Mohican nation who were among the original inhabitants of what is now New York City, particularly in the areas of upper Manhattan (Harlem) and the Bronx.

Wine/wining – A type of dance involving rotating hip movements, common in Caribbean dance.

Yuh – Dialect pronunciation of "you."

Acknowledgments

To my beloved husband, whose unwavering support and patience gave me the freedom to dive deep into this story — your love anchors me.

To my beloved sisters, thank you for giving me the grace to imagine a story that may weave fantastic threads from our shared experiences. Your love, understanding, and company have been the foundation for my creativity and courage.

To the Fellowship of the Griots, where stories flow like rivers connecting African descendants across oceans and continents — thank you for providing a sacred space where our voices can rise together. Your collective wisdom and support have been invaluable on this journey.

To Leora Alora, thank you for helping me open channels I didn't know existed and teaching me to listen when my ancestors speak. Your guidance helped me find my truth within these pages.

To my brilliant editors, Donald Weise and Crystal Nero, your incisive questions and keen insight transformed a tender flash fiction shoot into a flourishing prose garden. Thank you for seeing the potential and helping me nurture it.

To my incredible alpha readers who ventured into this story's earliest, rawest versions: Junior, Amanda Jones, Donnie Moreland, Teresa Brady and Mitch—your candid feedback, sharp insights, and steadfast belief in this project helped shape it in ways I never imagined. Your fingerprints are on every improved page.

Finally, to the readers and reviewers who will carry these characters and their stories in your hearts—thank you for completing the storytelling circle. Your engagement brings these words to life.

159

About the Author

Scarlet Ibis James crafts stories where Caribbean spirits intertwine with Harlem's rhythms, drawing deep from her Trinidadian roots and her life in New York City. Her latest novel, "Scarlet Birthright: What They Left Behind" (2025), emerged from her acclaimed collection "Scarlet Yearnings: Stories of Love and Desire" (2024), when readers and characters alike demanded their voices be heard.

Known for weaving intergenerational tales that pulse with soca rhythms and city beats, James explores how love, culture, and destiny reflect across oceans and decades. Her characters navigate the spaces between islands and boroughs, between traditional expectations and personal truth, creating stories that feel like conversations with your boldest friend – the one who understands that sometimes the bravest thing we can do is choose differently than those who came before us.

When not writing about love's many faces, James can be found hunting down the perfect roti in Queens, swaying to calypso in her Harlem apartment-turned-writing-sanctuary, or collecting stories while people-watching on subways and in parks. She believes every tale holds a touch of ancestral knowing, whether it blooms in Port of Spain's frangipani or poui trees or sprouts through the cracks of New York City sidewalks.

Her writing celebrates the complexity of Caribbean-American identity, the power of inherited stories, and the courage it takes to break cycles and forge new paths. For James, inspiration flows from everywhere – family histories whispered over morning coffee, steelpan rhythms floating on island breezes when she visits home, and the endless possibilities in her American city built where the spirits of the Wecquaesgeek people still rise.

Keep up with her at www.scarletibisjames.com.

More from Scarlet Ibis James

Scarlet Birthright: What They Left Behind (Audiobook)

In Scarlet Birthright, a forbidden summer romance ignites on Trinidadian shores — then ripples across oceans, generations, and hearts. Narrators **Le-Georgia Chambers and Richard Ragoobarsingh** *pull you into this lush, intoxicating world where one child's fate binds a fractured family. Long-buried truths, stone-cold sacrifices, and a legacy of undeniable love collide in this riveting island saga. Press play, and let the music of hope, regret, and redemption sweep you away. You'll listen, spellbound, until the very last word.*

→ Spotify | Audible | Storytel | Libro.FM | Google Play | Kobo, Walmart | hoopla | Audiobooks.com

What She Carried: Margaret's Story

Long before her role in **Scarlet Birthright: What They Left Behind** *opens with one impossible decision, Maggie is the woman who coaxes Joromi's restless fire into something bright yet never lets it scorch her spirit. From Port-of-Spain night markets to a Brooklyn winter that bites to the bone, Margaret rewrites the rules of marriage, motherhood, and immigrant ambition. And when fate tries to hand her the second-hand cloak of "stepmom," she refuses to wear it, choosing instead to stitch a destiny wholly her own.*

→ https://www.scarletibisjames.com | **Books**

Scarlet Yearnings: Stories of Love and Desire

A captivating collection of twelve intimate stories exploring the complexities of love, desire, and human connection. From tales of first encounters to destined bonds, each story reveals a distinct world of emotion and experience. This collection features "The First Time She Met Her Father," the poignant story that inspired the novella **Scarlet Birthright: What They Left Behind***.*

→ https://www.scarletibisjames.com | **Books**

Scarlet Yearnings: Stories of Love and Desire (Audiobook)

The stories are short but immersive, offering a perfect escape, whether you crave a quick indulgence or a deeper emotional experience. And the magic? It's in the voice. Narrated by **Jasmin L. Kirkwood***. Her sultry voice brings a warmth and irresistible intimacy, and the audiobook transforms each tale into a unique experience. Press play and let yourself be swept away.*

→ Spotify | Audible | Storytel | Libro.FM | Google Play | Kobo, Walmart | hoopla

Rhythms of the Soul: A Motivational Journal to Cultivate Gratitude and Inner Strength

This journal combines poignant quotes from Scarlet Birthright with extraordinary prompts for self-discovery and motivation. Unlock a more profound sense of purpose, heal old wounds, and cultivate the power of daily gratitude through guided meditations. This unique workbook has coloring pages, powerful affirmations, empowering exercises, and journaling pages. Begin writing a new chapter of inner peace and strength today!

→ https://www.scarletibisjames.com | **Books**